CW00504914

Critical c
I'm Dreaming of a Wilde Christmas

'My only regret is reading this book in mid November,
but that's just me - I love Christmas and it can't get here
soon enough! For those who can wait; wrap up warm
by the fireplace next to your Christmas tree, grab
yourself a glass of mulled wine and read this book. If
you are into romantic comedies and you are into
Christmas you will not be disappointed. It is
wonderfully funny, full of warmth and with great
characters and captures the spirit of Christmas nicely.'

Sarah Coldwell – Goodreads

Special thanks to:

Carol, Hannah & Amy

Copyright © Rhona T Pinkleton 2012

RhonaT@gmx.com

The right of Rhona T Pinkleton to be identified as the author
of this work has been asserted by him in accordance
with the Copyright, Designs and Patents Act 1988.

All rights reserved. No part of this publication may be reproduced,
stored in a retrieval system, or transmitted in
any form or by any means, electronic, mechanical,
photocopying, recording or otherwise, without the
prior written permission of the publisher.

This book is sold subject to the condition that it shall not, by way
of trade or otherwise, be lent, resold, hired out or otherwise
circulated without the publisher's prior consent in any form of
binding or cover other than that in which it is published and without
a similar condition including this condition being imposed on the
subsequent purchaser.

All characters in this publication are fictitious and any resemblance
to real persons, living or dead, is purely coincidental.

Digital edition first published in Great Britain in 2012
by Shotgun Publishing Ltd.
Company No. 06203678

Paperback edition first published in Great Britain in 2016
by Shotgun Publishing Ltd.
Company No. 06203678

ISBN: 978-0-9561253-2-3

Front cover design copyright © Rhona T Pinkleton 2012

I'm Dreaming of A Wilde Christmas

Rhona T Pinkleton

Chapter 1

It was one week before Christmas and snow had settled on a small rural town in South East England. It had created the perfect atmosphere for the festive season: Children were outside building snowmen and sliding down hills on their sledges. The shops were rammed packed with Christmas shoppers and that particular year, the local council had exceeded their budget with street decorations - spectacular lights hung across the roads and between the lampposts. An impressive Christmas tree stood in the centre of the shopping square - adorned with silver baubles, red ribbons and 3000 twinkling candle lamps. Christmas carols played through the Tannoys in the Square. The town was enwrapped by the spirit of Christmas.

But in a small cottage, not too far from the town centre, 67-year-old Jack Harris was seated with his legs up in a reclining chair in front of the TV looking as miserable as sin. His lounge had been beautifully decorated; the walls were adorned with Christmas cards, holly and tinsel, paper chains ran across the

1

ceiling and a beautiful Christmas tree sat in the corner. But it wasn't Jack who had captured the spirit of Christmas in his home.

As he sat, growing increasingly agitated, he could hear the whirling noise of a vacuum cleaner and the cluttering of plates, pots and cutlery from within the kitchen. Jack sighed heavily and looked up to the heavens in despair. He was clearly irritated by the housework that was going on in the adjacent rooms. Suddenly everything went quiet and Jack let out a sigh of relief:

'Hallelujah, praise the Lord,' he said quietly to himself.

His 38-year-old son, David, daughter-in-law Mandy and nine-year-old grandson Lance entered the room and promptly started fussing around him; tidying papers, rearranging furniture and opening the curtains.

Jack thought the world of his family and he normally looked forward to seeing them. But that Christmas was different: Up until then, Jack had been the picture of health - full of energy and vigour, he had such enthusiasm for life and lived it to the full.

But from his son's perspective, Jack always had too much on his plate – too many hobbies and social events, and way too many nights out at the local pub for his liking. Without actually saying the words "I told you so," David was noticeably irritated that his father's health had taken a turn for the worse, especially after having repeatedly told him that he should slow down in his old age. There was clear resentment in the fact that he now felt a responsibility of caring for his father, a lot sooner than he thought he would.

Since the passing of his wife, ten years ago, Jack had got used to doing things for himself and was irritated by the fuss being made around him – he hadn't asked for it and was unappreciative of it. There was an underlying friction between father and son.

Mandy put a newspaper and some magazines down by Jack's side:

'There's your newspaper and mags; have you got your glasses, Dad?' she asked.

'Yes, I have my glasses,' said Jack, listlessly.

'Here's the remote for the TV, Granddad,' said Lance.

Jack forced a smile:

'Thank you, Lance, you're a good boy.'

'I've put your food on the top shelf of the fridge and we've done all your washing,' explained David.

'Lovely,' said Jack. 'Did you scrub all my smalls?' he asked, jokingly. 'Or shall I nip out and buy six brown pairs?'

'Dad!' exclaimed David, unamused.

Mandy and Lance couldn't help but laugh, and Jack winked at them:

'Well, you know what it's like with us old folk.'

'I don't want to hear it, thank you,' said David.

'Skid-marks halfway up our backs,' Jack continued.

''Dad!' snapped David.

Mandy laughed out loud; she could see that Jack was just winding her husband up:

'Behave yourself, Dad,' she said, and gave him a kiss on the forehead.

'Now here is your new cordless phone,' said David with an edge. 'You understand how it works?'

'Yes, yes, it's not rocket science, David,' replied Jack.

'And you know where to put it to recharge?' continued David.

Jack was irritated:

'Yes, I shove it up my...'

'Dad!'

'On the base, I shove it on the base,' said Jack.

David was beginning to boil over. He turned away with his hands on his hips and legs astride, looking up at the ceiling, trying to regain his composure.

'Yes,' said Jack with a deadpan expression, 'he does Superman impressions, you know.'

Lance thought his Granddad was hilarious and was very fond of him. He came and sat beside him:

'Know any good jokes, Granddad?'

'Clean, please,' added Mandy, her eyes glancing over to David, who still had his back turned.

'Well,' said Jack, anxious to vex his son further. 'There were two nuns in a bath…'

'Right that's it!' said David.

'He's just winding you up, David,' said Mandy, placating.

Jack was smirking and waggling his eyebrows at his son.

'Oh, big joke,' said David, unimpressed.

Lance thought it was very amusing. Mandy sat beside Jack:

'Now are you sure you like what we've done with the Christmas decorations?' she asked.

'Love 'em,' replied Jack, earnestly.

'And the paper chains?' asked Lance. 'I made them.'

'Fantastic,' replied Jack.

'Okay, Dad, we're all done here,' said David.

'Blimey, David; do you have to make visiting me sound like a chore?'

'Sorry, Dad,' said David, knocked off guard. 'I didn't mean to.'

''Course it isn't a chore,' said Mandy, reassuringly. 'We love seeing you, Dad.'

'Yeah, Granddad,' added Lance.

Jack smiled and gently nodded in acknowledgement of the sentiment, but wasn't completely convinced about his son.

'Are you sure you don't need a blanket?' asked Mandy.

'Positive, Mandy, Thank you,' replied Jack.

'We've really got to run,' said David, looking at his watch.

There was a heartfelt group hug with kisses.

'Bye Dad, look after yourself,' said Mandy.

'I will, don't worry.'

'Bye Granddad, love you.'

'Love you too, Lance,' replied Jack.

As Mandy, Lance and David headed towards the door, David stopped and looked back.

'You won't forget your appointment at the hospital, will you Dad?' asked David, calmly.

'No, David, I won't forget.'

'Okay. Call me if you need anything, okay?'

'Okay,' replied Jack, with attitude and fed up again.

David looked at his Dad with concern and reluctantly turned away with his family.

The front door closed. The house was silent. Jack let out a sigh of relief. He sat in his chair for a few seconds tapping his fingers in boredom, then picked up his new cordless phone and dialled a number:

'... Hello, Harry. Fancy a pint?' asked Jack.

Chapter 2

Jack opened his front door and braced himself for the cold snowy weather outside. He was wearing a grey overcoat, a brown scarf, hat and black leather gloves. He closed the door, stepped out and stopped in his tracks; there she was, walking down the footpath towards her home - it was his next door neighbour Gladys Wilde. There was something about her that made Jack go weak at the knees. Gladys was 58 years young - she certainly didn't look her age. She was always well turned out; her hair was golden and immaculately styled, her make-up was fresh and flawless, her clothes and shoes were stylish and all designer labels. She was slim and attractive and had a grace about her. Even the way she walked, carrying a bag of shopping, oozed class - Jack always thought that he was way out of her league. But Gladys always managed to get him hot under the collar, to the point that he would turn into a fumbling idiot in front of her.

Jack stepped out into his open porch and stood next to a garden wall which had a number of flowerpots perched on top. He plucked up the courage to speak to her:

'Hello Gladys,' he said with a tremor.

Just as Gladys glanced over, Jack lifted his hand to wave and suddenly sent one of the flowerpots flying - *WHACK!* The pot crashed to the floor and shattered. Jack nervously smiled and waved. Gladys looked over and wasn't impressed, nor did she seem interested in idle chatter. She didn't break stride, but acknowledged Jack's existence:

'Jack,' she said, raising her eyebrows.

'Isn't it a glorious...'

Gladys had opened her front door and disappeared inside.

'...day?' finished Jack, looking somewhat embarrassed and dejected as he heard Gladys' front door close. 'If you like smashing flowerpots and freezing your nuts off,' continued Jack, mumbling to himself.

He kicked the broken fragments of the pot to one side, turned up the collar of his coat and ventured out into the snow.

On the quaint village road, towards the town centre, 76-year-old Harry Macdonald stood waiting. Harry was a tall stout man and as strong as an ox. He was wrapped up warm in a long coat and had a scarf wrapped around his neck. He was gently stamping his feet to keep warm. Harry was a happy-go-lucky character, with all the time in the world, never in a hurry to do anything, always cheerful and always joking - his dry sense of humour was often misunderstood by many, but it had rubbed off on his good friend Jack after many years of friendship.

Harry saw Jack tentatively approaching - carefully placing each step down hesitantly through the snow.

'You took your time,' said Harry, amused by Jack's walking technique. 'How many times did you fall on your arse then?'

'Not funny, Harry,' replied Jack. 'It's bloomin' slippery - I nearly killed myself back there.'

'Suicide?' quipped Harry. 'Did you bring a gun just in case you slipped and couldn't get up then?'

'That's just for horses, Harry.'

'Oh… I didn't realise horses can shoot themselves.'

'Good point. I suppose that's why they cover them up first in the Grand National, so you can't see them commit suicide.'

'Of course,' said Harry nodding his head in agreement.

'But suicide isn't the answer, you know?' said Jack.

'Yeah, you're right,' replied Harry, 'a pair of snow boots would be the answer.'

'How do they differ from normal boots?'

'Well, you only wear them in the snow.'
'Oh,' said Jack, content with the reply.

'Either that, or just carry a packet of salt with you,' suggested Harry.

'Salt?'

'Yeah, then just before each step, you throw a handful out in front of you.'

'Bloomin' heck, Harry; how big would my pockets need to be to walk into town?'

'Well, obviously you're gonna have to move closer.'

'Obviously,' said Jack, with a wry smile '... to a house five foot away,'

Jack continued carefully treading with Harry, who walked normally alongside him, unperturbed by the slipperiness of the snow.

'Now, Jack; if you feel yourself falling,' said Harry, reassuringly, 'grab hold of me…'

'Really?'

'…and I'll break your arm,' continued Harry.

'Gee thanks.'

'No problem. So anyway, why are you so eager for a pint?'

'I had to get out of the house,' explained Jack. 'I swear that boy of mine thinks he's swapped roles with me. When the hell did he became my father, Harry?'

'Kids are all the same, Jack. That's why it's so important to beat them as often as possible while they're young.'

'Oh, that's where I went wrong then; I never raised a finger to David... felt like raising a couple today though. Nag, nag, nag, nag, nag.'

'Ahhh he means well.'

'I know he means well. I just wish he'd mean well via the telephone... my new cordless telephone.'

'Cordless?' said Harry, impressed. 'I wonder what they do with all those unwanted cords?'

Jack was bewildered: 'Oh, that old chestnut,' he said sarcastically.

'Do you think they turn them into cord-uroys?' pondered Harry.

'Yeah,' said Jack, bemused, 'that's it.'

'Hmmm,' said Harry, pondering with intrigue.

'And another thing...' said Jack.

'Another thing?' wondered Harry. 'What was the first 'thing'?'

'I was just coming to that.'

'Oh.'

'Without so much as a by-your-leave; David decorated my lounge!' ranted Jack.

'You said it needed decorating.'

'Not that sort of decoration; Christmas stuff. You know; tinsel, baubles, tree, lights...'

'Action!'

'All those flashing lights - didn't even ask if I was epileptic.'

'Are you?'' wondered Harry

'No!.. Thank you for asking,'

'You're welcome.'

'...And please, no flash photography,' jested Jack.

'Okay,' agreed Harry. 'You know, you'll feel a lot better with a stiff one inside you, Jack.'

'Pervert.'

As they walked, at a painfully slow pace up a hill, they were approached by a young boy on a skateboard who was making his way down at speed.

'Well, that looks bloody dangerous to me.'

'Harry?' said Jack with suspicion, knowing him all too well.

Harry and Jack moved aside to allow the boy to pass. But as he was upon them, Harry smiled and purposely slipped out a leg. The skateboard hit it and the boy flew headlong into a pile of soft snow that had gathered at the roadside. Jack rolled his eyes; he expected something like that would happen.

Harry immediately rushed to assist the lad up:

'You okay there, nipper?' he asked, feigning concern. He picked the boy up and began brushing him off with unnecessary vigour. 'You're likely to do yourself an injury, young rascal.'

The frozen boy was stunned:

'I'm okay, I'm okay,' he insisted, unsure of what had just occurred and anxious that Harry should stop brushing him down.

Harry was suddenly proud of the boy:

'Ahhhhhhh, more courage than a Yorkshire brewery,' he said, and gave him a friendly but over zealous punch across the jaw.

'OW!'

Harry instantly broke into song:

'..*Much is that doggy in the window.*' Harry laughed out loud. He then reached into his coat pocket and produced some loose change. 'There you go sonny, a shinny penny; go get yourself a gobstopper.'

Jack rolled his eyes again. Harry roughly ruffled the

baffled boy's hair and slapped the penny into his hand. He then grabbed the skateboard, turned it up the right way and aggressively dragged the boy back onto it.

'Anchors away!' shouted Harry, as he pushed the shocked boy back down the hill. Harry then saluted the boy, in true military style, and rejoined Jack on their journey.

'Ah, they don't make 'em like that any more,' said Harry, admiringly.

'What? Full of bruises and broken limbs?' said Jack, bemused.

'Yeah, a dying breed.'

'Well, they would be… with you around.'

'Bless 'em,' said Harry, laughing.

Jack looked over to Harry:

'So, what did you get then?' he asked.

Harry produced a Bus Pass with a photo of the boy's round, chubby face on it:

'Hmmm a Bus Pass.'

'Got one of those,' said Jack with disappointment. Anything else?'

Harry produced a Nintendo 3DS game consol from within his pocket and looked at it with confusion:

'One of these,' he replied.

'Mmmmm... interesting,' said Jack. 'What is it?'

'Dunno - a mini computer type thingy,' explained Harry, screwing up his face. 'Probably does things like blood pressure, ECG, cholesterol levels.. and a rectal thermometer.'

'Lovely... You're not going to try it, are you?'

'Who knows, Jack, who knows?' replied Harry with his normal dry wit. 'I think that's why it used to be called a "Game Boy", you know.'

'Filthy pervert,' mumbled Jack in jest as they continued towards the pub.

Chapter 3

'The Dog & Trumpet' was a beautiful thatched roofed cottage pub that stood on a quiet country lane just outside of the town centre. Inside, it was very cosy and traditional. There were low beams on the ceiling and a real log fireplace. It was also decked out tastefully with Christmas decorations. A pine Christmas tree stood in the corner, adorned in gold baubles, red tinsel and twinkling lights. Harry and Jack were seated at a table near the roaring fireplace and were midway through drinking their pints of real ale.

'You see, the thing is, Harry,' said Jack staring into space, 'I do love them.'

'Yeah, I love 'em too,' said Harry. 'Are we looking at the same thing?'

'My son and his family.'

'Oh,' said Harry, 'I was looking at that woman over there with the big...' Harry stopped in mid sentence and started looking around. 'Are your family here then?'

'No,' replied Jack, 'I was just thinking about them.'

'Oh, I see!' said Harry, 'I thought you'd gone all Dorothy Stokes on me.'

'I really would like to think that David wants to see

me when he visits.'

'Doesn't he?'

'I dunno,' replied Jack. 'Mandy and Lance are fine, but David can't wait to leave, always checking his watch and will use any excuse to get out once they've finished their itinerary.'

'Is that a new Apple product?'

'What? The i-tinerary?'

'Yeah.'

'I suppose,' said Jack in puzzlement. 'Almost feels like he has an obligation,' he continued.

'Ahh come on, Jack, you're not being fair.'

'You don't think so?'

'Naa, he's probably doing it because he doesn't want you to change your Will.'

'Oh, that really makes me feel better, Harry,' said Jack with heavy sarcasm.

'Any time, Jack,' said Harry with a wink, downing a large mouthful of beer.

Jack also took a swig and sighed heavily afterwards.

'Okay,' said Harry, 'now we've got the family saga out of the way, what's really on your mind?'

Jack thought for a moment before replying:

'I've done it again.'

Harry was puzzled:

'That can only mean you've done it before,' he said - miffed at Jack's vagueness.

'Yes... every time in fact.'

'Oh!' said Harry in realisation, 'Now we're getting

to the nitty-gritty; it's Boris!'

'Boris?'

'Gladys … what's her face?!'

Jack stared into space, despairingly:

'Yes, Gladys Wilde.'

'What Norman Wisdom-esk type act did you inflict upon her this time?'

'I said 'hello'… and tried to wave…'

'…And set fire to her corset?'

'No; I smashed a flowerpot.'

'Oh, the old flowerpot ritual,' said Harry, nodding his head in recognition. 'I do believe they did that in ancient Greece as a form of greeting.'

'She wasn't impressed.'

'Different culture, you see.'

'She gave me a scornful look.'

'She would have kissed your feet in Athens.'

'But she did say my name.'

Harry was taken aback:

'What;.. 'Tosser'?'

'Jack!'

'Oh, Jack,' said Harry. 'Well, what are you so miserable about?!'

'I can't do anything right around her, Harry; I turn into a bumbling nincompoop!'

'Harsh words, Jack' said Harry shaking his head in despair. 'But at least she said your name, that's a start.'

'Start of what?'

'Whatever it is you're hoping to start.'

'I'm not sure I'm hoping to start anything.'

'Trust me Jack, if you're gonna turn into a jittery twit every time you see Boris Karlof, then you're hoping for something... and it ain't a knitted cardigan.'

'Will you stop calling her Boris Karlof!?... And a knitted cardi' would come in handy right now,' said Jack, calmly, warming his hands in the fireplace.

'Amen to that,' agreed Harry, raising his glass.

Jack raised his and they touched glasses and downed the rest of their pints.

At that moment, the pub's landlord, 55-year-old Stanley Bateman, approached. Stan was from the West Country, hugely overweight, with a large beer-belly, and always out of breath. He was extremely cheerful and friendly, but not the brightest of people.

'Afternoon gents,' said Stan. 'Have you seen the weather?'

Jack and Harry were puzzled.

'Yes, Stan,' said Jack, 'we came in from outside.'

'Is it possible to see weather?' queried Harry

'Good question,' replied Jack.

'They reckon there will be a heat wave to end all heat waves,' said Stan, dramatically.

Harry and Jack looked at each other in confusion.

'Are you sure, Stan?' asked Jack

'Oh yes, parts of Africa are having a really hard time,' explained Stan, 'hose-pipe ban and everything. There's folk out there that can't even wash their cars or nothin'!'

'It's terrible when you can't even wash your 'nothings',' said Harry.

'Tell me about it,' said Stan.

'Please don't,' said Jack.

'Anyway,' said Stan, 'it may not be Africa outside, but at least we'll all be sleepin' safe in our beds tonight.'

Jack thought for a moment:

'Is that because there are no lions around here?' he asked, tentatively.

'No', said Stan, bluntly, and puzzled by Jack's ridiculous question. 'It's because they caught that cat burglar.'

'I didn't know there was a cat burglar,' said Jack.

'Oh yes,' said Stan, 'bugger's stolen loads of cats in the neighbourhood.'

Harry contorted his face in bewilderment:

'That's not the definition of a cat burg…' Harry saw Stan's vacant expression. 'Never mind,' he continued.

'Someone was stealing cats?' asked Jack, in bafflement.

'Not any more,' explained Stan, 'they've got him!'

'Hooray!' said Harry, unenthusiastically.

Stan picked up the empty glasses from the table:

'They also said it will be 140 degrees in the shade later this week.'

Jack and Harry were bemused again.

'Won't catch me in the shade then,' said Harry.

'Me neither,' said Stan.

'I take it we're still talking about Africa?' asked Jack.

Stan was confused, 'Don't know,' he replied, 'I can't remember what we were talkin' about… or it might be that I just wasn't listening.'

'Yeah,' said Harry, wearily, 'one of those two.'

'But you'll be pleased to know,' continued Stan, 'that I've ordered a new pool.'

'Pool?' puzzled Jack

'… table. You didn't let me finish,' said Stan.

'Oh, sorry,' said Jack.

'That's alright,' said Stan, smiling broadly, 'accidents will happen.'

'True,' said Harry. 'Take that flowerpot incident today.'

'Leave it, Harry,' said Jack, unamused.

'Flowerpot,' said Stan, laughing for no reason. 'Nice one, I can take 'em or leave 'em, me-self.'

Stan held the empty glasses up: 'Any road: Same old, same old, gents?'

'Same old, same old, Stan!' came the reply in unison.

'Right you are,' said Stan, and waddled back towards the bar to fetch the drinks.

Jack suddenly remembered something important:

'Oh, don't forget, Harry…'

'I won't.'

'I haven't told you what you shouldn't forget yet.'

'Oh, sorry.'

'Don't forget to remind me not to forget my hospital appointment.'

'Hospital appointment?'

'Don't remind me,' said Jack, suddenly depressed.

Chapter 4

Gladys and her best friend, Wendy Glover, were in a coffee shop, sitting at a table with a mass of shopping bags by their feet.

'Well, that's it; at least we've got all the shopping out the way,' said Gladys, exhausted.

'Not quite,' said Wendy, 'we've still got to get you a dress.'

'I'm not sure about this,' said Gladys, sheepishly.

'For goodness sake, this isn't an arranged marriage.'

'I know,' said Gladys. 'But the trouble is I know you too well. You're on some sort of mission to hook me up.'

'Nonsense,' said Wendy, brushing off the suggestion. 'It's just a Christmas Ball, I don't even know if Andrew will be there.'

'Andrew?' said Gladys in bemusement. 'Who the hell is Andrew?'

'The man I'm going to introduce you to.'

'Last week it was Philip.'

'Oh him,' said Wendy, suddenly remembering. 'He's not your type.'

'Really?' said Gladys. 'After hyping him up for days on end?

'I wouldn't say days… weeks possibly.'

'And how, exactly, do you know what my type is?'

'Well, one that isn't getting married next February, that's for sure.'

'Oh,… I see,' said Gladys, 'yes I suppose Phillip isn't my type.'

'Told you,' said Wendy, teasingly.

'So tell me about this…'

'Andrew; what can I say? He's recently divorced.'

'Oh no,' worried Gladys. 'So he's an emotional wreck.'

'Don't be so pessimistic,' said Wendy.

'Sorry,' said Gladys, insincerely. 'Pray continue.'

'He loves the outdoors.'

Gladys quietly groaned:

'Hmm. Meaning; his house is a tip.'

'And he's got a bubbly personality.'

'Oh dear, you mean, he's fat?'

'He's larger than life.'

'He's overweight.'

'He's got a lovely smile.'

'He's a tub of lard.'

'Okay!' said Wendy in surrender. 'So he's got a few extra pounds here and there.'

'What on earth do you mean 'here and there' - London and Birmingham?'

'Well, some here...' said Wendy, pinching the skin on her waist, 'and some... spread out evenly everywhere else.'

'Hmmm,' groaned Gladys with suspicion. 'Sounds a dreamboat.'

'I'm not doing him justice,' said Wendy, defensively.

'You're certainly not doing him any favours.'

'Will you stop trying to read between the lines, Gladys; he's a very nice man; hard-working, charming, polite, not too tall, good head of hair...'

'Wait! What was that last one?' asked Gladys with concern.

'Head of hair?'

'No, back one; not too tall, you say?'

'Well,' said Wendy, knocked off guard, 'he's a little bit shorter than me.'

'Great,' said Gladys, sarcastically, 'and you're a little bit shorter than me! Which makes him a... 'Corbett'!'

'Oh come on Gladys, as long as you don't wear heels...'

'And he stands on a box?'

'...you should be fine!'

Gladys sighed heavily:

'Is that really the best you can do, Wendy?'

'I don't mean to be rude, Glad; but women our age can't afford to be too fussy,' said Wendy, caringly. 'Men aren't exactly coming out of the woodwork - like they were when we were in our teens.'

'I know,' said Gladys who paused to think. 'So can't you get me one of those teens then?' she said in jest.

'Listen, if I find a young stud that likes a woman our age, he'll have to go through me first!' joked Wendy.

The pair laughed. Gladys sat back in her chair and looked admiringly at her friend:

'Seriously, Wend; I appreciate what you're trying to do,' she said with sincerity, 'but I'm really not looking.'

'I know you're not looking, Gladys,' said Wendy in frustration, 'that's why I'm looking for you! And please don't give me that nonsense that you enjoy being on your own.'

'Well,.. I do.'

'No, you think you do, but there must be times where you miss having a partner?'

Gladys sighed again:

'Okay,' she said, holding her hands up in surrender, 'there are times.'

'See?' said Wendy, smugly.

'But they are just "occasional times",' insisted Gladys.

'Okay,' said Wendy, with a smile. 'So let's find you an "occasional" partner.'

Gladys sniggered and shook her head in defeat.

Wendy picked up her coffee and was about to drink when she suddenly thought of something:

'Gladys; it is a man you're looking for, isn't it?' she asked sheepishly in jest.

'Yes!' snapped Gladys.

'Just checking,' said Wendy, laughing to herself as she drank her coffee.

Chapter 5

Jack and Harry had just left the pub and were trekking through the snow, slightly the worse for alcohol.

'Okay, Harry, I give up,' said Jack.

'Ahh you should never give up, Jack. That's almost like... quitting.'

'Similar. You know, you've never failed to make Christmas... memorable; so what tragic fate awaits me this week, I fear?'

'Hmmmm Christmas you say?' said Harry, deep in thought.

'You're not going to give me that "I completely forgot" nonsense; are you, Harry?'

'Hmmm "nonsense" you say?'

'Why am I quivering in my boots?'

'It's the snow, Jack; your feet must be freezing.'

'Yeah,' said Jack, deeply suspicious of Harry, 'that will be it.'

'It's very inconsiderate, you know?'

'I can't help walking so slowly, Harry, and I've just had a few jars.'

'I meant Christmas coming just as the shops start getting busy,' said Harry, 'what on Earth was Jesus' mother thinking having him at that time of year?'

'I have no idea, Harry - I don't think I was born at the time.'

'Were you not?' said Harry, feigning surprise.

'She's younger than me, you know?'

'Only by 2000 years.'

'I meant Gladys.'

'Oh, Boris,' said Harry, rolling his eyes. 'I wouldn't worry.'

'No?'

'Naa, a lot of young women like older men,' explained Harry.

'Not my age, surely?'

'You'd be surprised,' said Harry, 'look at Hugh Hefner.'

'Crying out loud, Harry; Hefner is a multi millionaire and owner of Playboy.'

'Yeah, but I'm sure he likes older men.'

Jack sniggers for once, appreciating Harry's dry wit.

'But seriously…' said Harry.

'Seriously?' questioned Jack.

'Okay, maybe not "seriously"' said Harry, 'but let's face it, Jack; there's lots of wrinklies out there with younger crumpet.'

'You have such a sweet way with words, Harry; sheer poetry.'

'It happens, Jack,' said Harry. 'It's a fetish – some even like all them with flabby skin folds.'

Jack screwed his face up in disgust:

'Yuck.'

'It gives them sexual pleasure… and somewhere to put the remote control when they're not watching telly.'

'Oh…' said Jack, baffled. 'Maybe there is an upside then.'

'So you've got nothing to worry about,' reassured Harry.

Jack looked at Harry in puzzlement:

'Just for the record, Harry; I haven't got any of those flabby skin folds… yet.'

'Shame.'

'And you know when I said "younger"?'

'Phorr now you're going back, Jack,' replied Harry trying to recollect in jest.

'Gladys is just a "few" years younger,' explained Jack. 'I'm not exactly 'sugar daddy' material to her.'

'Once again… Shame.'

Harry suddenly spotted someone walking tentatively towards them:

'Look Jack!' said Harry, animated. 'I do believe that's Elsie Botherington, desperately trying to cross the road.'

There was an old and frail woman, in her mid-eighties, with a walking stick, hobbling along at a very slow pace towards them. There were hardly any cars around, and she was certainly not trying to cross the road.

'Poor old sausage,' said Jack with concern. 'We better go and help.

'Right you are.'

As they approached, Jack and Harry stopped either side of her.

'Elsie my dear,' said Harry, 'how the devil are you?'

'Elsie?..I'm not El...'

'We saw you trying to cross the road,' said Jack. 'You must have been waiting for hours!'

'Honestly, you'd think some bugger would stop, wouldn't you? added Harry. 'BASTARDS!'

The old woman flinched:

'Oh!' she cried, sweetly in shock. 'But..I wasn't trying to cros...'

'Here let us help you,' insisted Jack.

Harry and Jack grabbed an elbow each and steered the old woman into the road.

'But I don't want to cr.. !!'

'Aren't you glad we came along?!' said Jack, interrupting her.'

'You'd still be waiting, if it wasn't for us,' said Harry, 'wouldn't you? You old nutter.'

The old woman was irritated and confused:

'Will you let me...!'

'..make us a cup of tea?' said Jack, butting in. 'Very kind of you, but there's no need.'

'We're just happy to help, aren't we, Jack?' said Harry

'Happy as Harry!' replied Jack

Jack and Harry man-handled the old woman through the dunes of snow that had gathered at the roadside.

'I think my feet are getting...!'

'Better?' asked Harry. 'That's good; nasty things them bunions.'

'That and them traffic wardens,' said Jack, as they marched her across the road.

'Do you still get traffic wardens on feet 'round here then, Jack?' asked Harry, baffled.

'More often than you think, Harry.'

They landed the disgruntled woman on the other side of the road.

'Well, really..!!!' said the woman in distress.

'Now you just put your purse away, Mrs Botherington!' said Harry with authority. 'We didn't do this for profit!'

Harry and Jack started to walk away.

'Isn't she just the sweetest thing?' remarked Jack.

'Adorable,' agreed Harry.

'Threw away the mould.'

'And kept the cheese.'

'Totally,' agreed Jack.

As Harry and Jack continued wading away through the snow, the old lady slowly tried to make her way back across the road.

'Ohh! Ahh!' she cried out, in a tuneful way, unsteadily on her feet as she slid across the snow.

'And she sings musical numbers as well,' said Harry, not looking back.

'Multi-talented, I'd say,' said Jack.

After a short moment, Jack looked over to Harry:

'So, what did you get then?'

Harry started to empty his coat pockets:

'Uhmmm another bus pass... half a packet of Humbugs....'

'Lovely.'

'Oh, and a hearing aid.'

'Always useful.'

'You heard it here first.'

'Absolutely.'

'Humbug, Jack?'

'Why, thank you, Harry.

Chapter 6

Later that day, Jack and Harry had arrived at the small local hospital and were seated in a waiting room with six other patients. Whilst Jack was sitting patiently, with his arms folded and sucking a Humbug, Harry was in the seat next to him, wearing the oversized hearing aid on his left ear, frantically pressing the buttons on the Nintendo consol with excitement. The game's volume was cranked up full - the sound of futuristic laser shots and explosions ringing out. Jack was unperturbed by Harry's behaviour and was aimlessly staring into space, Gladys still on his mind. But the other patients were clearly agitated.

'Die you mother!....ship...die!' shouted Harry.

The receptionist was on the phone and trying to have a conversation. She was growing increasingly annoyed and she had heard enough:

'Sorry, can I call you back later?... Thanks', she said, and put the receiver down.

She approached Harry with a face like thunder:

'Could you turn it down please?!' she said with annoyance.

'Mister who?!' replied Harry, feigning deafness.

'NO, DOWN! COULD YOU TURN IT DOWN!?' she yelled.

'Brown?! I'm not Brown!' shouted Harry, who turned to Jack. 'You Brown?!'

Jack calmly shrugged his shoulders and shook his head. Harry jumped to his feet:

'IS THERE A BROWN IN HERE!!' he bellowed.

'DOWN! DOWN!' screamed the receptionist.

She snatched the Nintendo from Harry's hand, turning it every which way looking for the volume control. Harry grinned, sadistically as he watched her struggle. The receptionist was getting hot under the collar:

'Ohhh!' she said in frustration, before eventually finding the right button and muting the machine. 'There!' she said with relief.

She handed the consol back to Harry, who quickly turned his grin into a frown.

'Isn't that better?' she said, angrily.

Harry looked at his watch and leant in close to her:

'Half past three!!' he shouted, causing her to flinch.

The receptionist walked away shaking her head with annoyance.

Harry calmly sat back down. He looked at the Nintendo's display and was suddenly riled - his game had disappeared.

'HUMBUG!!!' shouted Harry with frustration.

Jack produced the bag of Humbugs from his pocket and offered them to Harry.

'No thanks!' said Harry, loudly, still pretending to be hard of hearing.

He turned to a male patient sitting next to him:

'Nearly choked on a damn Humbug once!' explained Harry. 'It got stuck, had to swallow it whole!'

The patient was unnerved:

'Really?' he said, uninterested and hoping the conversation would end there.

'Came out the other end looking exactly the same!'

Jack forced a wry smile.

'Identical!' continued Harry, at the top of his voice. 'I compared them!! Two Humbugs, couldn't tell them apart!!'

'Very odd,' said the patient, who was growing evermore uncomfortable.

'Very confusing!!' said Harry. 'Oh yes...I think I ended up eating the wrong one!...IT TASTED LIKE SHI....!'

'THAT'S QUITE ENOUGH!!' shouted the outraged receptionist,

'"FLUFF"?!!' said Harry, baffled. 'What are you on about, woman?!! SPEAK UP!'

At that moment, a nurse entered the waiting room carrying a clip board:

'Annie Schwortz?!' she called out, looking for her next patient.

'ANAL WARTS?' shouted Harry. 'That will be you Jack!!'

Harry slapped Jack on the back, who spat out his Humbug.

Chapter 7

Wendy was driving Gladys home. Gladys was sitting in the passenger seat with her head pressed against the window and staring aimlessly outside. She suddenly smiled and gently chuckled.

'What was that all about?' asked Wendy.

'Oh, just my neighbour,' replied Gladys.

'Who, Frank Spencer?'

'Yes, he's something else.'

'Ahh, do I sense a spark there?'

'You must be joking - I don't have enough insurance cover for a relationship with that man.'

'The bumbling buccaneer strikes again, eh?'

Gladys laughed out loud:

'I just don't know what it is with that man; every time I see him he either drops, trips or breaks something.'

'What did he do this time?'

'He said hello, and promptly smashed one of his flowerpots.'

'How?'

'I don't know! He just whacked it and sent it flying.'

Gladys and Wendy laughed together.

'I desperately tried not to laugh in front of him,'

explained Gladys, 'it wasn't easy.'

'How old is he?' asked Wendy.

'Not sure,' replied Gladys. 'A few years older than me, I guess.'

'What does he look like?'

Gladys was suspicious of the question:

'Do you know George Clooney?'

'Of course,' said Wendy, her face lighting up.

'Well, nothing like him,' joked Gladys.

'Ha ha,' said Wendy, unamused.

'I don't know why you were getting so excited, Wendy, you're married.'

'Only to my husband,' said Wendy, playfully. 'I'd be happy to negotiate the situation, should a George Clooney lookalike come along.'

'What? And you'd be happy to walk out on Brian?

'Who the hell is Brian?' replied Wendy. 'I'm still fixated on George, if you don't mind,' she said with a lustful sigh.

A short moment passed. Wendy was still curious about Gladys' neighbour:

'So...' she said, pryingly. 'Is he single'?

'George Clooney? How should I know?'

'Don't be flippant, you know exactly who I mean.'

'Yes, and I don't like where your questions are leading.'

'They're not leading anywhere,' said Wendy, defensively.

'Oh yes they are, little Miss Matchmaker,' said

Gladys, grinning.

'Mrs, if you don't mind... sadly.'

'I stand corrected.'

'So is he single - this neighbour of yours?'

'My God, I hope so,' said Gladys, 'I'd hate to think he's got a twin brother. Together, they could destroy this planet and every living soul on it.'

'I'll take that as a 'yes' then.'

'I don't know, Wendy,' said Gladys, mildly agitated. 'I haven't seen anyone resembling a wife or girlfriend going in or out of his house; but that might be because she's permanently based in the accident emergency ward of Saint Mary's Hospital.'

'You really don't like him, do you?'

'I never said that,' said Gladys, defensively. 'Jack's nice enough, I suppose.'

'Have you stopped to think that he's only a fumbling fool around you because he likes you?'

'Why would he like me? He doesn't even know me.'

'We'll maybe he likes what he sees,' replied Wendy. 'Let's face it Glad, you're a dishy lady... for your age.'

'Gee, thanks.'

'He probably thinks you'd be quite a catch.'

'....He'd probably drop me.'

Chapter 8

A short while later, Jack was seated inside the doctor's surgery. He had just finished a thorough medical check and was doing up his shirt buttons. Sitting close by was Dr. Stephen Pollard, a close family friend of Jack's.

'Jack, is there any point in me trying to give you advice?' he asked with concern.

'Probably not' replied Jack, blasé about his health issues.

'Well, I'm going to give it anyway,' explained Dr. Pollard, ''cause it's what I get paid to do.'

'How about I pay you more to keep schtum?' said Jack.

'Okay, well let me say this as a friend and not as a Doctor then.'

'Stephen, you've told me already. You've told me a thousand times.'

'And I'll keep telling you, you stubborn old scroat.'

'Is that a medical term?'

'Jack, I know you've been drinking; sucking a few mints isn't going to disguise it.'

'Humbug!' said Jack, imitating Ebenezer Scrooge. '...not mints.'

Dr. Pollard wasn't amused:

'I can't stress enough how serious your heart scare was,' he explained. 'You've got to take it easy. You've been given a second chance, some people aren't so lucky.'

'Well, that depends on your perspective, 'cause I don't feel lucky, Steve, in fact, I feel cheated,' said Jack in all seriousness.

'Cheated?' puzzled Dr. Pollard.

'Yes,' replied Jack. 'Take away all the things I love to do, and the things I love to eat and drink, and where does that leave me?'

Dr. Pollard laughed:

'Alive, Jack!' he said in disbelief. 'It leaves you alive.'

'No Stephen, it leaves me with no life at all.'

Dr. Pollard sighed heavily:

'Jack, I understand what you're saying, and I sympathize, but you can't expect to carry on like nothing's happened. Your body isn't functioning the way it used to. You have to make allowances.'

It was Jack's turn to laugh:

'Stephen, I'm 70 years old tomorrow. I could pop my clogs next week, or in 20 years time, it makes little difference.'

'Why?' asked Dr. Pollard in astonishment.

''Cause I've already lived the best years of my life. Can you understand that?'

Dr. Pollard paused to think, he knew there was some

truth in what Jack was saying and was sympathetic to the fact that Jack was ageing.

'But what <u>does</u> make a difference,' explained Jack, 'is not when I go, it's how; and I'm not going out confined to an arm chair eating soya beans and watching crap daytime TV.' Jack smiled defiantly.

Dr Pollard knew when he was defeated. He sighed heavily. Jack got to his feet.

'Call me, Jack,' said Dr. Pollard. 'The first sign of anything not right, just call me, okay? Can you do that much?'

'Okay, I'll call you,' assured Jack.

The two embraced.

Jack grabbed his jacket and coat from behind the chair. As he left the surgery, Dr. Pollard slowly sat - he was disturbed and concerned about Jack's health.

Chapter 9

Harry and Jack emerged from the hospital and began casually strolling back along the snowy footpath.

'So, what's the verdict?' asked Harry. 'Same old, same old?'

'Same old, same old,' replied Jack.

'Huh, doctors? What the hell do they know?'

Jack paused to think:

'Hmm,' he said. 'Nurses? They know a lot of nurses'.

'Yeah,...' said Harry, fantasising. 'Big, buxom, luscious nurses. Lucky devils.'

'Oh yes,' said Jack. 'And they get to examine all the "female patients". '

'You know what, Jack? I've just decided; when I die, I want to come back as a stethoscope.'

'Good choice,' commended Jack.

They turned onto a much quieter country lane and began to wade through fresh, untrodden snow.

'Harry, why do think funerals are such... morbid events?' asked Jack.

'I have no idea,' replied Harry, sarcastically.

'Well, I reckon it's the music. Those awful dismal dirges.'

'Enough to wake the dead, eh?' said Harry. 'I read somewhere that "Always Look on the Bright Side of Life" is becoming a popular choice nowadays.'

'Now that's more like it,' said Jack. 'Go out with a smile on everyone's face. Have you thought about what tune you'd like played at your funeral?'

Harry looked baffled:

'You're not planning to kill me, are you, Jack?'

'Not that I'm aware of,' said Jack. 'But the day's young.'

'That's a relief,' said Harry, unsure.

'So what's your tune then?'

'Tune?... Let me think now,' said Harry. 'I'm into the classics.'

'Forget the classics,' said Jack, 'you need something hard hitting, up-tempo and funky.'

'Like...?'

'Oooohh..anything... by Doris Day really.'

'Ah,' said Harry. 'Now you're talking - "I Can Do Without You" would be fitting, don't you think?'

'Perfect!'

'Mind you,' said Harry, 'it will probably sound crap on a 300 year old pipe organ, with some short-sighted Hallelujah bint on the pedals.'

'Organ?...Get modern, Harry,' said Jack with authority. 'They've got state of the art, fandangled, stereophonic hi-fidelity...thingies in churches now-a-days. You can drop any track and bomb the bass, Blood.'

'Really?' wondered Harry. 'What does that mean?'

'No idea,' replied Jack. 'Slap me some skin.'

'Slap your own skin,' said Harry in disgust.

Jack shrugged his shoulders; he had no idea what it meant either.

'Oh. Washing line at 6 o clock,' alerted Harry.

'You're kidding?' said Jack. 'Who leaves their washing out on a day like this?'

'Well, they've got to leave them somewhere,' said Harry. 'Follow me.'

'Rodger. Movin' in,' said Jack in military fashion.

Harry checked all around to see if the coast was clear, then led the way into a back garden through a side entrance, leaving heavy footprints in the snow as they walked. When they reached the line, Harry felt a black pair of boxer shorts that was pegged up:

'Blimey, I think they're dry,' said Harry in astonishment.

'Really?' questioned Jack. 'Probably silk then,' he explained. 'They don't take long to dry.'

'Excellent,' said Harry excitedly. He yanked them off the line and started to run towards a hedge.

Jack was bewildered:

'What are you doing?!' he asked, in a loud whisper.

'Trying them on,' said Harry, disappearing behind the hedge.

'Are you kidding?' said Jack in astonishment. 'You're gonna freeze your nuts off!'

'Mind over matter, old chum; mind over matter.'

Jack shook his head in bafflement and kept an anxious look-out while Harry started to get undressed.

'Bloody hell,' said Harry, shivering. 'Shut the door, Jack, there's a draught in 'ere,' he quipped.

Jack was nervously looking all around but couldn't help but quietly chortle. He could hear Harry's teeth chattering and the manic rustling noises coming from behind the hedge.

'Come on, Harry, hurry!' said Jack, trying desperately not to laugh out loud.

Harry popped his head out from behind the hedge in confusion:

'Harry Hurry?' he repeated. 'That doesn't sound right.'

'Get a move on!' said Jack through gritted teeth.

'Okay, okay; keep your pants on,' said Harry, and was back behind the hedge getting changed. 'I'm going as quick as I can.'

Jack could hear Harry gently humming and the sound of dripping water.

'What the hell..?' said Jack to himself in bewilderment.

Harry soon emerged from the hedge doing up his trousers. In his hand was a pair of dirty white Y fronts.

'About time,' exclaimed Jack.

'Sorry about that,' said Harry. 'I had to stop for a leak.'

'Great,' said Jack, rolling his eyes.

'I almost signed my name in the snow.'

'What?' said Jack, laughingly.

'Well, I did the 'H', 'A' and 'R' then ran out of steam… literally.'

'I don't wish to know that!' said Jack.

'Too late, I've already told you!' responded Harry.

Harry hung his old Y fronts on the washing line, where the boxer shorts used to hang, while Jack was still desperately trying not to laugh out loud.

'Nothing for yourself, Jack?'

'I'm alright for the minute,' explained Jack, 'David and Mandy did my washing.'

'Oh,' said Harry.

They hastily made their exit, back onto the road, where the pair laughed openly.

'Well, how are they?' asked Jack.

'Cold, Jack; numbingly cold.'

'No, really?' said Jack with heavy sarcasm. 'Who'd have thought?'

'They might even still be damp - too early to tell.'

'I hope you don't get frostbite, mate'

'Ooo, frostbite down in the South Pole region - wouldn't that be funny?'

'Yeah, hilarious,' replied Jack.

'Perfect fit 'round the waist, I must say.'

'Well, I'm glad you tried them on first.'

'Me too; not sure if they'd do 'returns''.

'I'm not sure if they did 'part-exchange' – but hey-ho.'

'They got a good deal,' explained Harry, 'that was

an old favourite of mine.'

'A hand-me-down family favourite, by the looks of them.'

'Yeah,' said Harry proudly, 'sad to see 'em go.'

'Still, 'got yourself a good deal there.'

'True. Mind you; bit loose 'round the two veg though.' said Harry, unashamedly adjusting himself.

'That's the style, Harry.'

'Is it?'

'Yes, lots of freedom, allows the tackle to breathe and swing freely.'

'You're not wrong there, Jack.'

Harry suddenly broke into song:

'*Swing low,...*'

Jack was quick to join in and together they sang at the top of their voices as they continued on their journey:

"*..Sweet chariot, coming for to carry me home!*"

Harry and Jack leisurely rambled through picturesque countryside, with rolling hills and trees glistening white with snow. The air was still and the sun had broken through the clouds; it was a glorious winter's afternoon to be out strolling.

Before long, Jack was tiring and slowed down.

'Hold on a sec, Harry,' he said, catching his breath. He sat down on the trunk of a fallen tree.

'You alright, Jack?' asked Harry with concern.

'Oh yeah fine,' replied Jack with a smile. 'I just

need a rest. We've done quite a bit of walking today.'

'Yeah, I suppose we have.'

Harry sat beside Jack. Their view was breathtaking with the snowy hills and valleys stretching off into the horizon.

'It's beautiful, Harry. When I think of all those years we used to drive everywhere. I'm almost glad they've revoked my licence.'

'I know what you mean,' said Harry, in awe of the view.

'Do you know, we've see more of the countryside in the last few months than ever before?'

'We certainly have, Jack... Still, it would be nice to have a motor, wouldn't it?'

Jack pondered for a moment.

'Yeah. But you're too old, and I'm too ill.'

'Only according to them bureaucratic scum bags. We know better though, right, Jack?'

'Right,' agreed Jack.

Jack pondered for a moment more:

'Harry, is there anything good about being old? I mean, anything at all?'

Harry had a good think:

'Uhmm.. A few quid off your heating bill, a free television licence... Oh, and a bus pass.'

'Yeah, terrific,' said Jack sarcastically.

'It's psychosomatic, Jack; I reckon we eventually become senile, old, useless gits 'cause everyone expects it of us.'

'They do, don't they,' said Jack in realization.

'And they go out of their way to make sure we turn out according to plan,' continued Harry with resentment. 'Taking away my bloody driving licence being a prime example.'

Jack tentatively got to his feet:

'You're right.'

'I know I'm right,' said Harry, also rising. 'You sure you're okay to continue?'

'As opposed to you leaving me to fend for myself in the middle of the forest? Oh yes.'

'Okay,' said Harry, admiringly. 'Here's a tip for you, Jack; if you're ever lost in the forest and you need to make fire, all you need is some dry twigs and leaves…'

'Yeah…' said Jack, dreading what was coming next.

'… some methylated spirit, lighter fluid, a gallon of petrol, a box of matches and a blow torch.'

'Thanks Harry, I'll try to bear that in mind.'

'I'm here to help.'

They set off again leisurely strolling through the countryside and enjoying every minute.

'You know, Jack, this is the sort of weather that's tailor made for an open-top sports car.'

'It would freeze your face off.'

'We'd have the heaters on.'

'Oh…right,' said Jack, in bewilderment. 'You know, I've always fancied a convertible Merc.'

'Now you're talking.'

'Harry, why don't you re-apply for a driving licence? You'd pass the medical hands down.'

'Principle, Jack, principle. No one, but no one is going to tell me when I'm too old to do anything.'

'Well, I admire your stubbornness, Harry.'

'Thank you, Jack.'

'Just out of interest; where are we heading?'

'I don't know. Shall we circle back to The Dog & Trumpet for a pint?'

'Yeah, why not indeed,' said Jack with enthusiasm.

Chapter 10

It was early evening. Wendy and Gladys were sitting in the back of a taxi on their way to the Christmas Ball. Outside, there was a full winter moon reflecting on the snow, transforming the landscape into a mesmerizing winter wonderland. Wendy was excited by the party while Gladys was in awe of the surroundings:

'Isn't it beautiful?' she said in a daze.

'Romantic,' replied Wendy, with a wry smile.

Gladys was suddenly apprehensive:

'Remind me why we're going again?'

'Cos we bought tickets,' replied Wendy, flippantly.

'Oh yeah,' said Gladys, wearily.

'Now cheer up, we're going to have a good time.'

'Yeahhhh,' sung Gladys softly with a deadpan expression.

'I've brought something for the journey,' said Wendy, raising her eyebrows and smiling.

'The cab fare home?' asked Gladys in jest.

'No, this…'

From out of her handbag, Wendy produced a small bottle of Bacardi, a bottle of Coke and two small plastic cups.

'So... you didn't bring the cab fare then?'

'Shut up,' said Wendy, good-humouredly. 'Now hold the cups while I pour.'

They arrived at the Black Bridge night club and a young doorman politely held the cab door open for the ladies to exit. It took a few moments for them to emerge, finishing off their drinks in a hurry and giggling like schoolgirls. The women interlocked arms and entered the club, showing their invitations at the door on their way in.

Inside, the women removed their coats, revealing Gladys' dazzling new blue dress.

'Look at you,' said Wendy in astonishment.

'Is the dress okay?' asked Gladys, worriedly.

'It's more than okay, you look gorgeous.'

'Thanks Wendy, you look pretty darn good yourself.'

'Thank you,' said Wendy, flirtatiously. 'Now, you're absolutely sure it's a man you're after?' she asked, pouting her lips and fluttering her eyelids.

Gladys tutted and rolled her eyes:

'No,' she said. 'But apparently that's why I'm here.'

'Right then, let's go and turn some heads,' said Wendy.

They left their coats in the cloakroom and headed into the main hall.

The ballroom was spectacular; it was built as a theatre in the 1930's and throughout the years it had maintained its traditional feel and look. But it was also decked out with wall to wall Christmas decorations and the ceiling was adorned with sparse twinkling lights that resembled the night sky. On stage, there was a big band "Glenn Miller Tribute" act, playing the swing hits of the thirties and forties. Everyone inside was suited and booted, and the place was heaving. Upon entering, Wendy and Gladys were immediately approached by a smiling waitress, attired in a traditional thirties dress, with silver tinsel around her neck and a Santa hat. She was brandishing a silver tray with champagne flutes. The girls helped themselves to a glass and made their way inside to mingle.

Chapter 11

Meanwhile, Jack's son, David, was at home and on the telephone. He was extremely worried. His wife Mandy was sitting close by, sharing David's concerns.

'Why doesn't he pick up the phone?' said David, panicking. 'Where the hell can he be? He should have been back from the hospital hours ago.'

'I'm sure he's fine,' said Mandy, trying to stay rational. 'Perhaps he's in the garden, or having a bath.'

'He's got a new portable phone that will work anywhere in his house – including the garden. Why doesn't he take it with him?'

'He's probably forgotten he has it,' said Mandy, in Jack's defence. 'You only bought it for him yesterday.'

'There are no other phones, Mandy; if he hears it ringing, surely he can follow his cars to find it?'

'Give him a break, David; maybe he can't figure out the buttons.'

David was beginning to boil over:

'Mandy, it's a great big green button with a picture of a receiver being lifted up – how can he not figure it out?'

'You know what old people are like.'

'Yes! Sadly I do. Honestly, he's worse than a child!'

David slammed the phone down. He instantly picked it up again and began dialling.

'Who are you calling now?' wondered Mandy.

'The hospital; 'make sure he actually got there!'

Chapter 12

Jack and Harry were seated at the bar with empty beer glasses in front of them. The pub's landlord, Stan, picked them up and held them aloft:

'Same old, same old, gents?' he asked with his normal beaming smile.

'Same old, same old, Stan,' said Harry and Jack in perfect unison.

'Right you are,' said Stan and proceeded to pour out the pints of draught bitter from a hand-pulled pump.

'What about good old Sam, eh?' said Stan, making conversation.

'Good old Sam?' wondered Harry.

'He's only gone and done it again, the old rascal,' explained Stan.

'Has he now, has he,' said Harry, bewildered. 'That's marvellous.'

Jack leaned in towards Harry:

'Who the hell is Sam?' he whispered.

'I have no idea,' replied Harry.

'Hey Stanley; who's Sam?' asked Jack.

'Holden,' answered Stan, surprised at the question.

'Samuel Holden?' asked Jack.

'The sheep-shagger?' added Harry.

'That's the one,' said Stan. 'Although we don't know that for sure, Harry.'

'Ah, come off it, Stan,' said Harry, insistently, 'the man's obsessed with his sheep. He never talks about anything else.'

'And he's not married,' added Jack.

'He is without doubt the strangest person I've had the misfortune of knowing,' said Harry.

'And the most boring,' continued Jack.

'Oh yes,' said Stan while laughing, 'he could bore the pants off a charging rhino at twenty paces.'

'Exactly,' said Jack, who looked over at Harry and they both shrugged their shoulders in confusion.

Stan served the pints out:

'There you go, gents.'

'Cheers,' said Harry. 'So, what has Sam done exactly?'

'He's only gone and won the South East Sheep of the Year contest,' answered Stan.

'I didn't think humans were allowed to enter?' said Harry, feigning puzzlement.

'Told you he was weird,' said Jack, reaching for his pint.

'No, no, no,' said Stan, 'not him personally; one of his furry friends.'

'Oh, wonderful,' said Harry, unimpressed.

'Apparently he won a cup... and one million pounds,' said Stan with astonishment.

Harry and Jack both spat their drinks out and choked in surprise.

'Are you sure?' asked Jack.

Stan thought for a moment and then suddenly remembered:

'Oh no... wait now,' he said, stroking his chin, 'that was the midweek Christmas lottery....that's right; Sam just won a trophy.'

'Well, bully for him,' said Jack.

'Anyway, he can tell you all about it himself, he'll be in, in a minute,' said Stan.

Harry and Jack looked at each other in horror.

'Cheers!' they said and touched glasses. They downed their pints in one, slammed the glasses down onto the bar and stood up.

'Right, we're off!' said Harry.

'Off?' puzzled Stan. 'Don't you want to hear Sam's story?'

'Absolutely...' said Jack.

'Not!' finished Harry. 'See ya.'

'Night, Stan,' said Jack.

'Oh,' said Stan, somewhat miffed, 'night boys.'

Jack and Harry had reached the door when it suddenly swung open. The men stood dead in their tracks in horror as 55-year-old Sam Holden, stepped in.

Sam was an enormous and scruffy six foot seven inch giant of a man who had an intimidating presence. He was carrying a framed photograph of his prize winning sheep, 'Stallion', under one arm and a trophy in the other. Sam was blocking the exit.

'Harry! Jack!' he said excitedly. 'You're not going anywhere,' he insisted, 'I'm buying you guys a drink!

Harry and Jack looked at each other with dread.

Chapter 13

Later that evening, inside the ballroom, Gladys was sitting alone at a table looking slightly the worse for alcohol. She wore a gormless smile as she downed another glass of champagne. At that moment, her equally drunk friend appeared, dragging somebody behind her.

'Gladys, found him!' said Wendy, her speech somewhat slurred. 'There's someone I want you to meet. This is Phillip!'

She dragged the man out in front of her and to the table. The gentleman held out his hand and smiled:

'Actually,' he said, looking quite embarrassed, 'the name's Andrew, Andrew Farrow.'

Gladys was pleasantly surprised. Through her drunken eyes, Andrew appeared a handsome man in his mid sixties, a little overweight, but looking good. He had a charming smile. Gladys accepted the hand:

'Gladys Wilde,' she said introducing herself. 'Pleasure to meet you.'

'And you too,' said Andrew.

'See!' said Wendy, smugly, her body gently swaying as she spoke. 'Did I tell you, eh? Did I tell you?' She bragged with an over-exaggerated wink.

'Yes, you told me,' said Gladys, her eyes fixed on Andrew.

'For he's a jolly good Farrow, eh?' continued Wendy laughing.

'Won't you sit down, Mr Fellow?' said Gladys.

'Farrow,' corrected Andrew. 'But please, call me Andrew,' he said and sat down at the table.

Chapter 14

Jack and Harry were propped up at the bar looking extremely fed up as they finished off the last drop of beer in their pint glasses. Sam was standing between them.

'...So, anyway,' said Sam, busy telling them about his trophy, 'that got me through to the quarter final stage. Old Stallion here was ecstatic, weren't you my darling?' said Sam, staring admiringly at the photograph.

Harry and Jack looked at each other in despair.

'Well, it was a wonderful story, Sam,' said Harry, anxious to get away.

'Oh, it gets better!' said Sam.

Stan picked up the empty glasses:

'Same old, same old, gents?'

'Same old, same old, Stanley,' replied Sam on the men's behalf. 'Keep them coming!'

Jack turned to Harry and winced.

'Right you are,' said Stan.

'So, the quarter finals....' continued Sam.

Harry and Jack lowered their heads in defeat.

A few pints later, Harry and Jack were looking

slightly the worse for alcohol, tired and extremely bored. Sam, however, was still full of energy.

'…But I'm telling you, one of the judges was a bit dodgy, to say the least,' said Sam, incensed. 'Stallion got through that round by just two points, when he should have won it hands down!' continued Sam slamming his hand down onto the bar - *WHACK!* Harry and Jack jumped.

'That's it!' said Harry, with bravado.

'That's what?' said Sam, towering over him.

'Errr I've got to... go to the toilet,' said Harry, cowering into an excuse. He got to his feet.

'Oh,' said Sam with disappointment.

'Yes!' said Jack, perking up and jumping to his feet. 'I've got to help him.'

'Help him?' wondered Sam.

'…err with him!' Jack fumbled, 'to the loo, if you know what I mean?'

'Oh,' exclaimed Sam, with more disappointment.

Sam stood watching Harry and Jack make a hasty dash for the toilet and shouted after them:

'Well, hurry back, got loads to tell you! Semi-finals next!'

Sam held the photograph of Stallion up and excitedly gave it a big kiss:

'You lovely, lovely boy, you!' said Sam.

Stan watched Sam with a nervous smile and obvious disgust.

''Ere Stanley...' said Sam, looking in the direction of

the men's toilets. 'Them boys are a bit weird, ain't they?'

Chapter 15

A few drinks later, Andrew was busy telling Gladys his life story and Gladys was decidedly drunk and somewhat bored. Her elbows were on the table with her hands propping up her head, she was having trouble focusing on Andrew's story and was distracted by the live band playing songs she adored. She was smiling and swaying to the music. Just to the right of her sat Wendy - slumped in a chair, too inebriated to move. She sat watching the pair with a smug, drunken smile.

'So, anyway,' said Andrew, 'she eventually took all the money out of our joint accounts and left that morning.'

'That's nice,' said Gladys, not paying any attention. 'So tell me Mr Fellow,.. Fallow, Mellow, Marrow; do you like the music of yester-year?'

'Er, yes very much,' said Andrew, 'I used to be quite the dancer, in fact...'

'Blah blah blah, she left you, yes I know,' said Gladys, rudely interrupting. 'You really need to move on, Mr Meadow.'

The song finished and there was a rapturous round of applause.

'Bravo!' shouted Gladys and started slapping her hand on the table.

The bandleader stepped up to the microphone:

'Thank you, Ladies and Gentlemen, sadly we're coming to the end of the evening...'

'BOO!!' shouted Gladys.

'...so this will be our final song of the night,' continued the bandleader. 'So please take your partners for 'Moonlight Serenade'.'

Another round of applause rang out.

'Oh, I love this, said Gladys, sitting back in her chair.'

As the music started, Andrew got to his feet and held out a hand:

'Could I have the honour of this dance, Ms Wilde?'

'Why, Mr Fatto, Flubby, Flabbo, I'd be delighted,' she replied.

Gladys staggered to her feet and looked around in puzzlement. Andrew was considerably shorter than Gladys, barely reaching her shoulders.

'Where have you gone?' she asked.

'I'm here,' said Andrew, coyly.

Gladys glanced down:

'Ah, little Timmy's fallen down the well,' said Gladys in her drunken stupor. 'Never mind, stand up and come with me.'

She took Andrew by the hand and led him out onto the dance floor. The pair looked an odd couple as they held each other and swayed gently to the foxtrot, with

Gladys towering over the tiny Andrew. Gladys closed her eyes and lost herself to the music, a heavenly smile on her face. In that moment, she didn't have a care in the world. But it was about midway through the song that the alcohol caught up on her and Gladys began to feel unwell. She opened her eyes and stop dancing:

'Oh dear,' she said, unsteady on her feet.

'Are you okay?' asked Andrew with concern.

'Sorry to cut this short... no offence,' apologised Gladys, 'but I think I need to go to the little boy's room... no offence. I'll be back... shorty... shortly.'

'None taken,' said Andrew.

Gladys abandoned Andrew on the dance floor and started to hobble away like Long John Silver - having left behind one of her stiletto shoes.

Andrew wasn't too sure what to do with himself and felt rather self-conscious to be standing amongst a sea of smooching couples dancing around him. But he suddenly spotted Gladys' shoe on the floor and picked it up.

'Who was that mysterious lady?' said Andrew to himself, smitten.

He held the sparkling shoe up with both hands in front of his face and, somewhat pervertedly, inhaled its aroma. He wallowed in the odour and blissfully exhaled:

'Whoever this shoe shall fit, I will...'

Before he could finish the sentence, the shoe was snatched from his clasp.

'Sorry, Stumpo,' said Gladys, 'I'm gonna need that for the long journey home.'

She then held her mouth, feeling herself about to be sick, and made a mad dash towards the toilets.

Chapter 16

Moments later, Harry was outside the pub helping Jack climb through a toilet window. Jack was having a hard time and Harry was desperately pulling at Jack's arms.

'Harry, will you stop pulling,' said Jack, in a strained voice. 'I'm caught on something!'

'Don't care,' said Harry, 'I'm not leaving without you.'

'I applaud your friendship, but my clothing is caught!'

At that moment, local man, 77-year-old Ray Hargreaves, mysteriously appeared beside Harry. Ray was a very laid back, slow and lethargic person. He had a pipe in his mouth and was pushing the tobacco down with his thumb. Ray was very softly spoken:

'Evening, Harry,' he said, unfazed by Harry and Jack's shenanigans.

Harry stopped tugging at Jack.

'Oh, evening, Ray,' said Harry calmly.

'Jack,' said Ray.

'Hello, Ray,' said Jack, who stopped struggling and just dangled limply from the lavatory window.

Ray casually lit his pipe, while Harry and Jack,

looking somewhat embarrassed, waited patiently. Ray took a few puffs and looked curiously at Jack hanging.

'I take it, Sam Holden's in tonight then?' assumed Ray.

Harry calmly nodded:

'Uh huh.'

'He.. err.. won some kind of trophy or other,' explained Jack.

'Oh dear,' said Ray.

'No, sheep,' said Jack.

'Oh, sheep,' said Ray.

'Yeah, bloomin' sheep,' said Harry.

'Oh,' said Ray.

Ray puffed on his pipe a few more times whilst he thought; blowing the smoke into the cold night air. 'Well, I won't keep you then,' said Ray, calmly. 'Thanks for the heads-up.' He lethargically walked away from the pub.

'Yeah, goodnight, Ray,' said Harry.

'Goodnight,' said Jack.

Harry and Jack patiently watched Ray walk off into the distance.

'Harry, get me out of here; I'm freezing!' said Jack. 'This isn't the way I thought I'd go!'

'Well, if you're gonna go, you're in the right place.'

'Just get me out!'

'Right,' said Harry, grabbing Jack's arms and tugging hard.

'Gently, Harry, gently,' pleaded Jack.

A loud *rip* was heard as Jack finally fell through the window, landing on the soft snow below.

'You okay?' asked Harry.

'I've just fallen out of a window, Harry!... 'Course I'm okay,' replied Jack, annoyed.

Jack stood up, revealing to Harry that his trousers were ripped around the groin area and his underwear was showing through.

'Ahh...The Scarlet Pimpernel,' said Harry, smiling.

Jack looked down:

'Ah, it's nothing,' he said.

'So I've heard,' agreed Harry.

Suddenly, Sam's voice was heard from within the toilet:

'Jack, Harry?!! Where are you?!!'

'Quick,' said Harry in a panicked whisper, 'spread out and head for the hills!'

'Right!' said Jack, then suddenly thought. 'Oh, fancy a Chinese?'

'You know I don't like all that foreign food,' replied Harry, affronted.

'Indian?' wondered Jack.

'Now you're talking,' said Harry, excitedly. 'Let's go!'

The two friends scurried off across the snow.

Chapter 17

Inside a busy and plush Indian restaurant, Harry and Jack were intoxicated and struggling to focus on the menu. There was a red rose in a glass vase on the table in front of them and napkins that had been neatly folded into the shape of a fan. Their coats were hanging on the back of their chairs. Jack and Harry swayed in their seats, in time to the sitar music playing in the background.

'So, said Harry, 'how are we gonna get you with this Boris girl then?'

'What on Earth made you bring her up?'

'This red rose; unless you thought it was for us?'

'I never thought anything of it.'

'Thinking about it,' said Harry, looking over his shoulder. 'I hope people don't think we're a couple of ballet dancers.'

'Ballet dancers aren't gay, Harry… are they?'

'Well, I wouldn't like to share a prison cell with one, if that's what you mean?... Although they would come in handy if you need to get something down from the top shelf – all that tippy toe stuff they do.'

'Anyway,' said Jack, 'how about we just have a nice meal and not even think about Boris... err Gladys.'

'Anything you say, Jack... anything you say.'

Jack stared at the menu, trying to focus.

'Besides, I've got no chance,' said Jack.

'Hmm?' said Harry, busy trying to scan the menu. What was that, sorry?'

'I'm talking about Gladys.'

'...Is that the... 'Gladys tikka masala' or the 'Gladys Dhansak'?'

'What?'

'Are you still going on about that woman?'

'You started it,' replied Jack.

'That conversation finished ages ago,' said Harry in bewilderment. 'Concentrate on the menu.'

'I can't.'

'Too much in love, eh?'

'No! I haven't got my glasses,' replied Jack.

'Oh.'

'And I'm a bit drunk.'

'Double 'Oh'.'

'Can I borrow your glasses, Harry?'

'They're in my coat pocket and I'm not getting up for anyone.'

'But you're wearing them.'

'Uh uh uh!' said Harry, waving a finger. '<u>Anyone</u>!' he emphasized. 'Now remember, Jack, you've gotta watch what you eat, so you let me do the ordering. Okay?'

'Okay,' said Jack, in surrender but unbothered.

Harry took the menu from Jack's hand and waved

over the Indian waiter, Raj, who came poised with an order pad and pen.

'Ah, Raj, my good man.'

'Yes, Mr Harry,' said Raj.

'Right so that's sausage, bacon, mushroom, egg and chips twice, and four slices of toast with butter, thank you' said Harry, handing the menus back to Raj.

'Any popadoms?' asked Raj.

'I'm Gladys you asked,' replied Harry, 'four popadoms and some sweet Wilde mango chutney'

'I know what you're doing, Harry,' said Jack, unimpressed.

'What's that?' asked Harry, innocently.

'You're trying to kill me with all that cholesterol!' Jack turned to Raj. 'I'll have margarine instead of butter.'

'Yes, boss,' said Raj. 'Anything to drink?'

'Oh yes,' said Harry, excitedly, 'two bottles of that tasty Boris brew please, Raj.'

'Newcastle Brown Ale?' asked Raj.

'That's the one!'

'Right you are, Mr Harry!'

'What a nice next door neighbour, he'd make' said Harry, with a wink to a bemused looking Jack.

Chapter 18

Gladys and Wendy were sitting in the back of a cab on their way home from the Christmas Ball.

Wendy was very drunk, but still smiling. Gladys was looking the worse for wear, her head resting on her friend's shoulder.

'How are you feeling?' asked Wendy.

'Oh,' sighed Gladys, pitifully. 'Okay,'

'Ahhh, poor baby,' said Wendy empathetically, putting a comforting arm around her.

'I feel terrible.'

'Too much of the old champers, eh?'

'No… well, yes, but I was talking about that little fella.'

'Andy Farrolli,' said Wendy in an Italian accent.

'Was that his name?' asked Gladys, contorting her face in confusion. 'I think I may have insulted him.'

'Ah, don't worry; he's got a good sense of humour, Glad,' said Wendy, reassuringly. 'Besides, it would have gone straight over his little head - which wouldn't be hard, let's face it.'

'Glad you can laugh.'

'Well, it is Christmas; tidings of good cheer and all that. So cheer up, Gladys.'

'Huh,' sighed Gladys, despondently. '*You* don't have to spend another Christmas alone.'

'Nor do you, you soppy tart,' said Wendy, laughingly. 'You're always welcome to come and spend Christmas with us.'

'Not that sort of loneliness.'

'Ohhhhh, bedtime, snuggles, type loneliness?'

Gladys softly sighed again – which answered Wendy's question.

Wendy slapped her hand on the back of the cab driver's seat:

'Excuse me,' she said in a slurred voice, 'are you single?'

'Oh my goodness,' said the 50-year-old driver in a broad Nigerian accent, 'I have five wives back in Abuja. Why?'

'Never mind,' said Wendy, angrily. 'Keep your eyes on the road… and not on the talent back here.'

'Thanks for trying, Wend,' said Gladys.

'No problem, Glad,' said Wendy, cradling her friend tighter.

'Five wives, indeed,' said Gladys, disapprovingly, 'I'd be better off with the walking disaster zone.'

'Would you now?' said Wendy, teasingly, knowing that Gladys was talking about Jack.

'Figure of speech, Wend.'

'Hmm,' said Wendy with suspicion.

'Oh, the horror,' said Gladys despondently in a daze. 'I'd have to have "Accident Claims Direct" as a speed dial number in my phone.'

'I know what would cheer you up; do you fancy an Indian?'

'Well, the Nigerian's already spoken for.'

'Not that sort of Indian.'

'Food?'

'Mmmm…vindaloo'

'Urgh,' said Gladys, grimacing. 'I've already been, thanks.'

'Go on,' urged Wendy, enthusiastically. 'Let's really give ourselves something to remember in the morning.'

'No thanks, Wend, I couldn't face suffering from both ends. I just need a hot cocoa and my bed.'

Chapter 19

Not long later, Jack and Harry were mopping up the last bit of food from their plates. They both collapsed backwards into their chairs – stuffed and very drunk.

'Ahhh, that hit the spot,' said Harry with satisfaction.

Jack was looking uncomfortable:

'Why do I always eat too much when I go for an Indian?'

'It's the spices.'

'Oh.'

Raj approached and placed the bill down onto the table:

'There you go, boss.'

'Thanks,' said Jack.

'I'll get this, Jack,' said Harry, grabbing the bill.

'Okay,' said Jack.

'What do you mean "okay"?'

'Uh?'

'You're supposed to say "No, I'll get this" and then we argue for a few minutes,' explained Harry, deeply insulted.

'Why?'

''Cause that's what friends do.'

'Oh... I see,' said Jack in bemusement. 'No, no, I'll get this,' he said in a lacklustre tone.

'Don't be silly, it's my treat,' said Harry, continuing with the act.

'No, no, I insist.'

'Okay, if you insist,' said Harry, passing the bill over.

'Eh?' said Jack, bamboozled.

Harry got to his feet and began to stagger away:

'I'll get our coats.'

'Coats?' said Jack in puzzlement. 'They're hanging on the back of our ch...'

'Tut tut tut!' said Harry. 'I said I'll get them.'

Jack shook his head in despair and looked at the bill. He found his wallet and slapped some cash down onto the table. Then, with a huge strain, he managed to get to his very unsteady feet.

'Thank you, Mr Jack,' said Raj, picking up the money.

'No, thank you,' insisted Jack.

As Jack was putting on his coat, Raj suddenly noticed the rip in Jack's trousers:

'Oh, I see you brought a little friend,' said Raj with a broad smile. 'Mind he doesn't catch cold.'

Jack was baffled by the remark. He shrugged his shoulders and removed the red rose from the vase on the table.

'Toodle pip, Raj,' said Jack

'Toodle pip, Mr Jack, replied Raj.

As Jack headed towards the exit door, he grabbed Harry's coat from behind the chair.

Jack stepped outside the restaurant to find Harry waiting for him, wearing an unfamiliar coat and carrying another.

'Oh, there you are, Jack; I've got your coat,' said Harry, holding out the one in his hand.

'Oh,' said Jack, puzzled, 'and I've got yours,' he said holding out Harry's coat.

'Thank goodness for that,' said Harry exchanging coats, 'it's bloomin' freezing out here.'

Harry proceeded to put his coat on, on top of the one he was already wearing, and Jack did the same.

'That's better,' said Harry. 'You look fantastic.'

'Thank you,' said Jack, too drunk to realize that he was wearing a bright green woman's coat that was way too small for him.

'Right then,' said Harry, 'I'm off home. What are you up to?'

'Same,' replied Jack.

'Okay see you tomorrow, Jack,' said Harry, walking off.

'Yeah, later, Harry,' said Jack.

Jack spent a moment struggling to pull the coat together to do up the buttons:

'Blimey I've put on weight,' he said to himself.

He quickly gave up and headed on home.

Chapter 20

It was late at night. Jack was staggering back towards his home, singing at the top of his voice The Carpenters song, "There's a kind of hush".

'*There's a kind of hush! All over the World Tonight!..*'

A few of the neighbourhood dogs had started to howl along with him and one irate neighbour could be heard shouting out of his window:

'Oi! Shut up, you idiot! Don't you know what time it is?!'

But Jack was blissfully unaware of the racket he was making, or his painfully out of tune vocal performance. He had just about reached Gladys' front door when his song reached the finale:

'*People just like us are falling in love!!*' sang Jack, sustaining the final note, with arms aloft, having placed the rose between his teeth, belting out the note at the top of his voice. Two more dogs were howling along in the background.

Gladys hadn't made it to bed. She had collapsed on the settee downstairs but was startled awake by the noise outside. She grabbed her dressing gown and went to investigate.

Jack was still belting out the final note when Gladys opened her front door. She was taken aback to see the sight of Jack, in his tightly fitted woman's coat, still holding his final dramatic pose. Gladys wrapped the gown tightly around herself:

'This is new,' she mumbled in astonishment.

Jack eventually ran out of puff, ending the final note. He slowly lowered his hands and removed the rose from his teeth, then gormlessly smiled at Gladys:

'Hello Rose,' he said in a slurred and drunken voice, holding out the flower, 'look, I've got you a Glad-iol-ys.'

'How thoughtful,' said Gladys, with a deadpan expression.

'I just popped out for a bit.'

'So I see,' said Gladys, staring at the rip around the groin area in Jack's trousers - his underwear clearly visible.

'Perfect night for an evening, isn't it?' said Jack looking up at the night sky.

'Shouldn't you be inside?' asked Gladys. 'The pair of you,' she added.

'Now, Gladys,' said Jack trying to be serious, 'there's a possibility I may do something stupid.'

'Nooo,' said Gladys sarcastically.

'Yes, yes, yes,' insisted Jack, 'cos I always do,' he said, gleaming with pride.

Gladys wanted to laugh but somehow managed to hold herself back:

'Go home, Jack - get yourself some sleep.'

'Oh no, no, no,' said Jack, affronted. 'Don't talk to me about sheep; that's how I ripped my trousers.'

Gladys was baffled, and slightly curious, but didn't want to ask:

'Sleep, Jack, Sleep!'

'Oh, shut-eye! That's good advice,' said Jack nodding his head. 'And I will! Just as soon as I find my...'

Jack started to pat himself down, searching all the pockets in the wrong jacket.

'Tampon!' he said, holding one up. 'There'll be no leakage tonight!!' he shouted at the top of his voice whilst waving a clenched fist in the air - setting off the dogs howling again.

A neighbour's voice suddenly burst out:

'Will you shut up?!!'

Gladys was struggling not to laugh:

'Go home Jack!' she insisted.

'Yes, I will,' said Jack. 'Because I'm worth it!' he added with a prolonged wink.

Gladys smiled to herself as she watched Jack stagger towards his house next door. He was still searching his pockets and started to sing softly in a deep voice:

'*Swing low, sweet chariot, coming for to carry me home.*'

Gladys stood at her front door, shivering in the freezing cold, waiting to see if Jack could make it inside. He wobbled along his garden path, taking two paces forward and one back, merrily singing, until he eventually disappeared behind his porch wall. Gladys then heard him shout:

'Ah, there's my lipstick!'

She shook her head in bafflement and went back inside when she heard Jack's front door open: It was opened by his son, David, who was stunned at the sight of his Dad.

Jack was swaying at the doorstep with badly applied lipstick, smudged across his face, and a rose placed behind his ear. David scanned his Dad's clothing in disgust; from the Norman Wisdom-esk tight fitting woman's coat to the ripped trousers and exposed Y-fronts. Jack was wearing a broad smug smile:

'Shhhh, don't go out there, David,' warned Jack in a drunken whisper. 'It's ladies night tonight and they've lost one of these.'

Jack held up the tampon by the string and promptly fell into his son's arms.

'We'll talk about this in the morning,' said David, through gritted teeth.

Chapter 21

The following morning, Jack was feeling like hell as he struggled down the stairs trying to tie his dressing gown together. His hair was a mess and there were still traces of lipstick smeared on his face. When he had reached the lounge, he stopped, surprised to see his son, daughter-in-law and grandson sitting quietly in wait.

'Hi, Granddad,' said Lance, tentatively.

'Hi, Lance,' replied Jack in a daze.

Mandy couldn't help but snigger at the sight of Jack.

'You're looking well, Dad,' she said, sarcastically.

'Thank you,' said Jack, scratching his head in confusion.

'Have you cut yourself shaving?' asked Lance.

'Not yet,' replied Jack, feeling his cheek and looking at the red smear on his hand with puzzlement.

'Dad, can I have a word please?' requested David, getting to his feet.

'Yes,' said Jack, rubbing his chin in befuddlement. 'I have questions; many, many questions.'

Jack followed his son into the kitchen and David closed the door.

'So, how are you feeling this morning?' he asked.

'Never felt better', said Jack, groggily. 'Feel like a 20-year-old... if you know of any? And a couple of paracetamols wouldn't go amiss.'

Jack started to search the cupboards for tablets.

'Do you want to tell me about last night?' asked David, calmly.

'Oh... I slipped on a bar of soap,' answered Jack aping a prison convict.

'Not funny, Dad.'

'I can't remember too much.'

'I'm not surprised, you were out of your head!'

'I may have had a drink,' said Jack, coyly.

'Dad, I don't even want to talk about your torn trousers, the woman's coat, the lipstick on your cheek or the lady's hygienic insert you were waving about…'

'That's good,' said Jack, mystified but slowly recollecting some of the events from the night before.

'My concern, Dad, was that you were out all day!' said David angrily. 'I rang the hospital and spoke to Stephen; he said you'd been drinking before you'd even got to him!'

'Oh, David, he shouldn't have said that; that's completely unprofessional.'

'Not according to Stephen - he said he spoke to you as a friend, not as a doctor.'

'Oh yeah,' said Jack, remembering. 'Crafty bugger.'

'Dad, why are you doing this?! Have you got a death wish, or something?'

Jack laughed sardonically:

'No, son. Don't be silly.'

'I'm glad to hear it.'

'I'm Gladys to say it.'

'You're what?'

'Nothing,' said Jack, mystified as to why he said it.

David began to calm a bit:

'I worry about you, Dad - we all worry about you. We don't want you to go to an early grave.'

'I know,' said Jack, with understanding.

'Then why are you doing this to yourself, and your family?'

'David, it's Christmas, will you give me a break? I've got to have some enjoyment.'

David took a moment to consider and felt he might be pushing his Dad too far. He reluctantly changed the subject:

'What are you doing for Christmas Eve?' he asked, 'Mandy and I would love to take you out; maybe we could get some last minute tickets to a show, or the movies or something.'

'Ahh, that's nice, David, thanks. But I've reserved it for Harry.'

'Harry MacDonald?' asked David with concern.

'There's only one Harry.'

'You're not wrong. Dad, the man's a nutcase!'

'Yes, he's a lot of fun, isn't he?'

'That's not what I meant.'

'Don't worry, we'll probably just have a quiet glass of sherry somewhere.'

'Hmm...' said David with suspicion.

Jack located the headache tablets and poured

himself a glass of water. He was about to take them when he stopped:

'Oh,' he said panic-stricken, as he suddenly remembered his encounter with Gladys the night before.

'What's wrong?' asked David with concern.

'Nothing,' said Jack, with a tremor.

Chapter 22

Gladys was in her dressing gown and was sitting at the kitchen table - feeling and looking like hell. There was a cup of coffee in front of her that she tried to pick up, but the smell was too much and she promptly plonked it back down and pushed it away, groaning in disgust.

The phone suddenly rang and Gladys jumped out of her skin. She had to cover her ears before finding the handset and answering:

'Hello,' she said, groggily.

'Are you up?' asked Wendy, as right as rain and busy pottering around in her kitchen.

'Barely,' replied Gladys, 'and do you have to ring so loudly?'

'Oh,' said Wendy, 'a bit on the delicate side, I take it?'

'No no,' said Gladys, sarcastically. 'I just need a hole to collapse into and I'll be fine.'

'Ooo, that bad, eh?' said Wendy, sympathetically. 'Well, I've got something to cheer you up.'

'Cyanide capsules?'

'Nope; Andrew called me this morning.'

'Andrew?' said Gladys, racking her brain. 'Remind

me?'

'Andrew Farrow,' said Wendy in disbelief, 'the man I introduced you to last night.'

'Oh yeah… vaguely,' said Gladys, unsure. 'The one that was standing in a hole?'

'What?' said Wendy, laughing in bemusement.

'Yes,' said Gladys, recollecting, 'I seem to recall meeting one of Santa's little helpers.'

'Okay, Gladys, so he was a bit on the short side.'

'A bit?' said Gladys, bemused. 'Wendy, I have short skirts taller than him.'

'That's a bit of an exaggeration, isn't it? I thought you two were getting on like a house on fire.'

'All he wanted to do was talk about his flipping wife!' exclaimed Gladys. 'Apparently she's going to get everything - including the house. I was so bored, I felt like going 'round and setting fire to it, to save him the misery... so I suppose you were half right.'

'Well, he certainly took a shine to you,' said Wendy. 'He's asked if he can have your phone number.'

'You didn't give it, did you?' worried Gladys.

'Of course not,' replied Wendy, 'I gave him your home address.'

'You didn't,' said Gladys, bolting upright.

'Joke!' said Wendy. 'I thought that might wake you up. Now go and get yourself ready, I'll be 'round later.'

'Oh, okay,' said Gladys in a daze.

Chapter 23

Later that afternoon, by coincidence, Jack and Gladys emerged from their homes at the same time. As they began to walk up their garden paths, Jack was filled with dread and embarrassment. In a somewhat childish way, he quickly hid his face with his hand, blinkered from Gladys as he walked. Gladys was wondering how much Jack had remembered of his performance the night before and Jack hiding his face suggested he remembered quite a bit. Gladys smiled and called across:

'Good morning, Jack.'

'Morning,' said Jack, reluctant to uncover his face and picking up pace.

Jack was so anxious to get away that he swiftly walked from his garden and turned sharply, straight into an elderly woman out walking her Yorkshire terrier. He collided with her, sending her into a privet hedge. When Jack went to help her, he accidentally trod on the terrier's paw. Her yappy dog started growling and barking at Jack. Gladys stood watching in disbelief as Jack backed away. The woman got to her feet:

'Why don't you look where you're going?!' she said angrily.

'Sorry,' said Jack, still backing away.

He glanced over to Gladys and nervously smiled, then walked into the road without looking. An approaching car tooted and slammed on its brakes. It skidded along the road and gently nudged Jack's legs before screeching to a halt - sending the thick layer of snow, on its roof, flying off into Jack and covering him. Fortunately, Jack wasn't hurt and waved at the driver, signalling that he was okay. The angry motorist looked daggers at Jack and mouthed profanities.

'Sorry,' shouted Jack, who brushed himself off and hastily continued across the road.

Gladys was shaking her head in bewilderment:

'Unbelievable,' she quietly mumbled to herself.

Chapter 24

A short while later; Jack had met up with Harry. They were casually rambling through picturesque countryside that had been transformed by the snow into breathtaking scenes of beauty.

'Honestly Harry,' said Jack in despair, 'I've never been so embarrassed.'

Harry was smirking; he couldn't help but find Jack's misfortune highly entertaining:

'And you serenaded her, you say?'

'Yes - if that's what you can call it.'

'Exposing yourself and dangling woman's hygiene products at her?'

'Yes, Harry,' replied Jack, agitated. 'I've got a woman's coat at home with all sorts of goodies! I'm a walking boutique.'

Harry momentarily looked away and chortled quietly to himself.

'God, it's so embarrassing,' continued Jack, 'I tried to hide my face when I saw her this afternoon'.

'Oh, you saw Boris today; did she say anything?'

'I didn't give her the chance; I was too busy pushing old biddies into hedges and treading on their mutts.'

'Ah, the old distraction ploy.'

'Yeah... worked, I managed to get away... after being hit by a car,' mumbled Jack.

'What?' said Harry, chuckling. 'You really are Frank Spencer.'

Jack groaned:

'And if that wasn't bad enough, this morning David gave me a right dressing down!'

'Excellent, I could use one of those myself.'

'What?'

'A nice dressing gown.'

'No Harry, a dressing down! He told me off - like I was a teenager.'

'Ah, you're his only living parent, Jack - he's bound to be overprotective.'

'Do you think?'

'Sure; he does it out of concern... Cos you're old and useless.'

'Gee thanks, Harry.'

Moments later, Harry and Jack were sitting on a bench that overlooked a river with stunning views of the snow covered hills.

'Harry, do you miss Valery?'

'Who the hell's Valery?'

'Your wife...?'

'Oh, that Valery... I forgot about her.'

'Seriously, Harry.'

'Seriously, Jack? I guess there isn't a day that passes that I don't think about her. She was a one off.'

'Can't argue with you there, Harry; she was a lovely woman.'

'Well, I wouldn't say 'lovely'... I probably wouldn't even say 'woman'. But I loved her, Jack, I loved her.'

'I know,' said Jack with compassion.

'How about you, do you still miss Vicky?'

'Ahh, it was a very long time ago, Harry.'

'But you never met anyone else.'

'I met plenty.'

'Plenty?'

'Well... one. But I guess I wasn't ready to jump into another relationship.'

'How about now?'

'Now... I think I'm too old.'

'You're never too old, Jack.'

'Who the hell would want a decrepit 67-year-old man? And please don't say 'a decrepit 67-year-old woman'.'

'I was going to say Boris, but your answer's much better.'

'Boris?' laughed Jack, sardonically. 'I wouldn't be surprised if I got home and there was a 'for sale' sign up on her garden gate.'

'Who the hell would want to buy a garden gate this time of year?'

'Ha ha... It's a nice gate, as it happens.'

'Really?' said Harry, pondering. 'How much is she asking?'

'I'll let you know,' replied Jack, straight-faced.

'Thanks.'

Harry was looking somewhat uncomfortable and started scratching his private parts.

'Harry, do you have to play with yourself while you're talking to me?'

'I think I may have been bitten,' explained Harry, continuing to scratch.

'Bitten?'

'You know - bugs, Jack.'

'Bed bugs?'

'Probably, I was bitten three times last night, once right on the end of my... you know what.'

You're kidding? said Jack, with a broad grin.

'Don't make me prove it, Jack, it ain't a pretty sight.'

'So I've heard.'

'It's these boxer shorts - anything can crawl up there. There's enough room to squeeze in a family of rabbits.'

'Now that's just perverted,' said Jack, getting to his feet. 'Come on, let's keep walking - take your mind off it.'

'Good idea, said Harry.'

Moments later, Jack and Harry were rambling through the snow across a field, alongside a wire fence, when they heard a distant voice coming from behind them:

'JACK, HARRY!'

'Uh oh,' said Jack, 'that sounds like Sam.'

'Don't turn 'round,' said Harry, with alarm. 'Keep walking, we didn't hear him.'

'Right,' said Jack, picking up the pace.

'HARRY, JACK!!' bellowed the voice again.

'He's gaining on us,' panicked Jack.

'Well, walk quicker then,' ordered Harry.

'My legs won't go any quicker,' said Jack.

'If I have to hear about his prize winning sheep again, so help me I'll...'

The voice was on top of them.

'JACK, HARRY!!'

Sam reached out and pulled Harry back by the shoulder - forcing them to stop. They turned to face farmer Sam Holden, who was red-faced and out of breath. To Harry and Jack's horror, Sam was carrying his prize winning sheep, Stallion, under his arm.

'Oh.. hello Sam', said Harry, extremely fed up.

'Sam,' said Jack, wearily.

'What happened to you the other night?' asked Sam. 'You just disappeared.'

Jack hesitated: 'Err..' he said, fumbling for words.

Harry was quick to jump in:

'Jack had a bit of an accident,' he explained. 'In the... err men's room.'

'That's right,' agreed Jack, playing along.

'Oh?' said Sam, momentarily baffled, but suddenly thinking that he knew what had happened. 'Oh, right, got it' said Sam. 'Don't worry, Jack, it happens to me when I've had a few.'

'Does it?' wondered Jack.

'Oh yeah,' replied Sam. 'Peed all down your leg did you? Had to rush home change your trousers?'

'No!' said Jack, affronted.

'Ahhh!' said Sam with a smile. 'You must have caught your pecker in your zipper; done that a thousand times, me.'

'Have you?' asked Jack, in astonishment.

'Stings a bit, but hey!' said Sam, with a wink. 'It's only a pecker!'

Jack and Harry glanced at each other in disbelief.

'So anyway,' said Sam, excitedly, 'where was I? Oh yeah, Stallion in the semis...'

Harry lowered his head and winced.

Hours later, Sam was still talking enthusiastically about his sheep, while Harry and Jack were shivering in the cold and looking extremely fed up.

'...So anyway, I said Stallion *is* a prize winning sheep,' said Sam, pointing a finger, 'I want at least two hundred quid if you want to mate them, and he said "fine"!'

'Yeah.. great,' said Jack, unenthusiastically.

'Just like that!' said Sam, smugly. 'Honestly, didn't even try to haggle or nothin'. I could have asked for anything. Two hundred was the first figure that came to me.'

'Yeah.. great,' said Jack, unenthusiastically again.

'I tell you, I was kicking myself all the way home,'

said Sam.

'Yeah.. great,' said Harry. 'Well, nice chatting to you, Sam. Riveting story. We've really got to...'

Sam ignored Harry and spoke over him:

'Next week, I'm taking Stallion to the national Sheep of the Year competition,' he said excitedly.

'Oh, enjoys watching that, does he?' asked Jack, unimpressed.

'Watching?' said Sam in puzzlement. 'He's one of the favourites to win it. Look at him. A perfect specimen. Daddy loves you.'

Sam kissed Stallion on the head, while Harry and Jack looked on in disgust.

'So you're the father?' asked Jack, obnoxiously.

'Figure of speech,' explained Sam. 'Stallion and I...'

Harry had heard enough and interrupted with a loud cry:

'ARGHHHH!!!!!!!!!'

'What?' asked Sam, flinching backwards.

'Did you see that?' said Harry, clearly disturbed.

'See what?' wondered Sam.

'He sneezed,' said Harry.

'Sneezed? Who sneezed?' panicked Sam.

'Stallion,' said Harry, 'he sneezed.'

'I didn't hear it,' said Sam, who turned to Jack. 'Did you hear it?'

'I saw it. Looked like a sneeze to me,' replied Jack.

'Eh?' said Sam, examining Stallion's face with concern.

'His eye's look a bit glazed over, don't you think Jack?' said Harry, nudging him with his elbow.

'Yeah, I noticed that,' agreed Jack.

'His eyes?! Where?' asked Sam.

'Either side of his nose,' mumbled Harry with an edge.

'Oooo I don't like the looks of this, Harry,' said Jack.

'Oh no, what's happening?' said Sam, unsure what to do.

'You better get Stallion home, and straight to bed,' instructed Harry.

'Bed? Really?' said Sam.

Harry yelled again:

'ARGHHH!!!!!!!'

Sam flinched backwards and also yelled:

'ARGHHHH!!!!! What?!' he asked.

'He sneezed again!' said Harry.

'I saw it!' confirmed Jack. 'I definitely saw it!'

'Oh no,' said Sam, with a whimper.

'Don't just stand there,' said Harry. 'Run!!'

'Well, go on!!' said Jack.

Sam was in a state of shock. He nodded, turned and started running.

'Don't even stop for nothing!!' shouted Harry.

As they watched Sam heading off into the distance, Harry and Jack were feeling smug.

'That felt good,' said Harry proudly, whilst scratching his private parts.

Jack watched Harry, tutted and rolled his eyes. He turned and continued walking with Harry following.

'"Don't even stop for nothing"?' quoted Jack. 'What kind of English was that?'

'Worked for me,' said Harry.

'Hmm'

Chapter 25

Jack and Harry had approached a stream and up ahead they could see a man fishing.

'Ahhh, fishing,' said Harry, 'there's something we haven't done in a while.'

'That's 'cause you hate fishing,' said Jack. 'What was it you used to say again?... Oh yes "I'd rather shut my willy in the door".'

'Well, I'm older and wiser now, Jack.'

'Certainly older, Harry.'

As they drew near, the pair split up. Harry stood watching the angler from behind a bush, whilst Jack crept up to a car that was parked nearby. When he was in position, Harry gave a thumbs up, and Jack swung his backside against the car door - setting off a piercingly loud alarm.

The angler was up instantly:

'What the hell...?' he said, abandoning his fishing gear and going off to investigate.

Harry watched him leave with a broad smile.

The angler approached his car and turned the alarm off with a remote from his key. He briefly looked to see if the car had been broken into and thought nothing of it - car alarms have the tendency to set off frequently for no reason, especially out in the sticks where wildlife could be the explanation.

A moment later, the angler returned to his fishing patch and stopped in his tracks, horrified. All his fishing gear had vanished. He looked around, shocked and baffled - there was no one in sight.

Harry and Jack leisurely meandered alongside the bank of the stream, carrying all the fishing gear - the rods slung over their shoulders.

'I'm not really looking forward to another Christmas on my own, Harry'.

'What brought that on?'

'Don't know.'

'Oh,' said Harry, knowingly, 'we're back to Boris.'

'I didn't particularly mean her, Harry.'

'But the lust of a horny woman?'

'There you go with that poetic tongue of yours.'

'Well, how would you put it?'

'The affections of the heart and soul, Harry.'

'Don't make me put my finger down my throat, Jack.'

'Sorry.'

'Besides, no matter how you sugar-coat it, we're back to the dilemma that is Boris.'

'She's not a dilemma, Harry; she's a 'no go'.'

'Don't be so hasty, my friend. Judging by your antics in the past few days, I think I may have misjudged her.'

'What do you mean?'

'I mean, that she can't be that bad,' explained Harry. 'She took the initiative and said hello to you this afternoon - even though you made a complete numpty of yourself.'

Jack took a moment to reflect:

'Yeah, she did, didn't she?'

'She's clearly got a sense of humour. I bet she's a right raver, when you get to know her.'

'Get to know her?' said Jack, rolling his eyes, 'I've got little hope of that. She looks down on men like me, Harry.'

'That's 'cause a woman like Boris needs to be impressed. They like chivalry and valour. You know, show her your manhood.'

'You show her your manhood.'

'I would, but it's a bit sore,' said Harry, scratching his private parts again. 'I tell you Jack, a woman needs to be given plenty of white rum and a night of passion.'

'Is this your 'Barcardi and Cock' joke, Harry?'

'Oh, you've heard it.'

'Hmm,' said Jack, frowning.

'This looks like a good spot,' said Harry, dropping the fishing rod and tackle.

'We're not actually going to fish, are we, Harry?'

'Why not?' said Harry, with a broad smile.

'Cos it's bloomin' freezing,' replied Jack.

Harry produced a small silver flask from within his coat pocket:

'Brandy, Jack?' he asked, raising his eyebrows.

'You truly are a fisherman's friend,' said Jack, smiling.

Harry and Jack were sitting on a log, fishing in the stream. They were focused and concentrating on the floats bobbing in the water.

'Well?' asked Jack.

'I'd still rather shut my willy in the door,' replied Harry, looking extremely bored.

'Maybe if you caught something, you'd change your opinion.'

'Yeah, right,' said Harry sarcastically. He took a swig of brandy from the flask and handed it to Jack.

'I'm hungry,' said Harry.

'Me too,' said Jack, who tried to take a swig but was mystified to find it was empty.

'You know, we'd actually starve to death if we were fishing to survive,' said Harry, with an exaggerated face of misery. 'How long have we been here now?'

Jack looked at his watch:

'Six minutes.'

'Oh,' said Harry. 'Seems longer... much, much longer.'

Jack's float suddenly pulled underwater and Jack was up on his feet with excitement:

'Get a fire started, Harry. Here comes dinner!'

'Really?' said Harry, up on his feet and sharing the excitement.

Jack struggled as he tried to reel in his catch:

'It's a whopper!' he exclaimed.

'Don't lose it, Jack. I'll get the net.'

Just as Harry returned with the net, Jack pulled up the rod, and their faces dropped with disappointment; there was a tiny fish wriggling at the end of the line – no bigger than the size of Jack's hand. They both stood watching it for a moment.

'Hmm,' said Harry. 'So when you said "whopper", were you saying it from the perspective of a Pigmy.. with a growth hormone deficiency?'

'Well...'

'Let's go to the pub.'

'Good idea,' agreed Jack.

Chapter 26

It was mid afternoon when Harry and Jack entered The Dog & Trumpet pub carrying all their newly acquired fishing gear. They approached the bar and Stan greeted them:

'Afternoon, gents.'

'Is he talking to us, or the lavatory?' said Harry in jest.

'Same old, same old?' asked Stan.

Harry and Jack simultaneously replied:

'Same old, same old, Stan.'

As Stan began to pour out the draught bitter, Harry noticed a poster on the wall behind the bar advertising a "Christmas Fair" coming to the town. Harry and Jack seated themselves on bar stools at the bar.

'I didn't know you're into fishing, Harry,' said Stan, puzzled.

'You didn't?' said Harry, with surprise.

'What was it you used to say about fishing?' said Stan, thinking hard. '... Something about a door?'

'No, Stan,' said Harry. 'I love it. LOOVVVEEEE it!'

'Yeah, I couldn't drag him away,' said Jack, straight-faced.

'Catch anything?' asked Stan

'You bet,' answered Harry. 'It was a monster.'

'A monster!' said Stan in horror, dropping a pint glass to the floor - *SMASH!*

All went quiet in the pub.

'Just a figure of speech, Stan,' explained Jack.

'It was just a bloomin' great fish,' said Harry.

Stan was unsure:

'So, you're saying it wasn't a monster?' he asked, fearfully.

'No,' replied Harry, 'just a fish.'

Stan let out a sigh of relief and smiled:

'Thank heavens for that,' he said, continuing to pull the pints. ''Ere, you gotta be careful. A guy came in here earlier...'

'Not an actual guy?' said Jack, mortified.

'Thanks for the warning, Stan,' said Harry, continuing the drama.

'No!' said Stan. 'This guy had a load of fishing gear when he went out fishing on the moors.'

'No?' said Harry, feigning surprise.

'Yes!' said Stan, not really understanding the concept of sarcasm. 'And he lost it all, whilst he was fishing.'

'Rather careless of him,' said Jack.

'No! It vanished,' said Stan in a scary voice, 'into thin air.'

Harry and Jack both pretended to be shocked, and gasped in unison.

'And,' continued Stan, 'he heard the sound of blood curdling screams and howling monsters.'

Harry and Jack's simulated stunned look turned into one of confusion.

'Did you just make that last bit up?' asked Jack.

'Who can tell, Jack?' replied Stan. 'When stories get passed around, the truth can sometimes be distorted.'

'Hmm,' said Jack, with suspicion.

Harry was looking uncomfortable and was shifting around on his seat.

'Stan, do us a favour', said Harry, 'have you got a long cool glass of ice water?'

'Something wrong with the beer, Harry?' asked Stan.

'No, it's not for me,' replied Harry. 'It's for.. er..'

Harry leant forward and whispered in Stanley's ear.

'John Thomas!!' said Stan, horrified; dropping another pint glass to the floor - *SMASH!*

The pub went quiet. Stan scanned the bar area:

'I thought I banned that little prick!' he said, angrily.

Chapter 27

Gladys opened her front door. She was dressed ready for the weather outside and carried a shovel. She put the door on the latch and began shovelling the snow on her garden path.

Having had a few beers, Jack and Harry, looking slightly the worse for alcohol and still carrying the fishing equipment, were walking back towards Jack's house. Harry suddenly stopped - he had spotted Gladys in her front garden.

'Hold it!' he said.

'What's up?' asked Jack.

'Isn't that Boris?'

'Oh my God, yes. Quick, let's hide,' said Jack, panicking.

'Now now, let's not be hasty.'

'You weren't there last night, Harry.'

'I'm not sure you were all there, Jack.'

'That's not the point. Come on let's go back to the pub.'

'Jack, calm down; I've got an idea.'

'I don't like it,' said Jack.

'You haven't heard it,' puzzled Harry.

'I'm not sure I need to.'

'Look, Jack, this is the perfect time to impress.'

'Impress?' worried Jack.

'Oh yes. Follow me,' said Harry, leading Jack away towards a side street.

'Wait a minute...' fretted Jack, trailing Harry and unsure what was going on.

Gladys was on the last patch of snow to clear from her garden path, when Harry and Jack reappeared, slowly walking towards her. This time there were three large rainbow trout hanging from Jack's rod, slung over his shoulder.

Jack's heart was pounding hard - he was a nervous wreck:

'This is ridiculous; she's never going to fall for it, Harry.'

'Yeah, she will. Just stick to the plan,' said Harry, coolly.

'Plan? What plan?'

'Oh,' said Harry in confusion, 'I thought you had a plan.'

'Me?!!'

'Look, she's probably spotted us now, so there's no turning back.'

'What do I do, Harry? What do I do?' panicked Jack.

'Just follow my lead.'

'I know I'm gonna do something stupid, Harry.'

'Thanks for the heads-up; do you mind doing it

now, instead of in front of Boris?'

'And don't call her Boris, Harry!' said Jack in a loud whisper as they approached.' It's Gladys; Gladys Wilde!'

'Okay, I've got it,' said Harry, unconvincingly.

'Oh God, I'm gonna have a panic attack and these fish weigh a bloomin' ton, Harry.'

'For goodness sake, Jack, they're only four pounds each, how does that amount to a ton?'

'Well, feel how heavy they are!'

'Shhh not now, Jack. Let me do the talking.'

They had reached Gladys' front garden and Gladys had stopped shovelling.

'Hello Ms Wilde!' said Harry, cheerfully. 'Merry Christmas!'

'Merry Christmas,' replied Gladys.

'I'm Harry - Jack's alter ego,' said Harry in jest - which got a dirty look from Jack in return.

'Pleased to meet you,' said Gladys, hospitably.

'Hello Gladys,' said Jack, coyly.

'Hello Jack,' said Gladys with a grin.

'Sorry if I startled you last night,' said Jack, timidly.

'That's okay; I'm glad you found your lipstick', said Gladys with a wry smile.

'Lipstick?' questioned Harry.

'Forget it,' said Jack.

'I'd rather hear the story, if it's all the same, mate,' said Harry.

'Er.. We've been fishing!' said Jack, distracting

them from that particular line of conversation.

'So I see,' said Gladys.

'Jack's a natural,' said Harry, 'I keep telling him he should enter competitions, he's championship material. Seen these?'

Harry swung Jack around so Gladys could see the fish.

'Less than an hour he took to catch that lot,' continued Harry, enthusiastically. 'Can you believe it? I never even caught nothing!'

Gladys seemed impressed, until she looked at the fish closely.

'Ain't that impressive?' said Harry. 'Huh?'

'Remarkable,' said Gladys, 'I know it's cold today, but how did you manage to catch three frozen fish?'

There was a stunned silence, then Harry let out a false laugh:

'No, no, he caught them this morning,' he explained, thinking up an excuse as he went along, 'and... we.. had to keep them on ice while we went for a celebration toddy! Ain't that right, Jack?'

'Oh,' said Jack in a lacklustre daze, 'yeah, we er.. buried them in the snow.'

'That's what we did!' said Harry, relieved at Jack's quick thinking.

'You're welcome,' muttered Jack, with a deadpan expression.

'Listen, we are going to have these beauties for supper,' said Harry, enthusiastically, 'Jack is an amazing cook. I mean, a real cordon bleu connoisseur'.

'I didn't know you could cook, Jack?' said Gladys, impressed.

Jack was bewildered:

'Neither d...'

Harry nudged Jack in mid sentence:

'Well, I wouldn't say connoisseur, exactly,' continued Jack.

'Ahh, you're too modest, Jack,' said Harry, patting him on the back. 'I've seen him cook a five course meal for a party of ten, and every one of them said it was the best meal they've ever had!'

Jack was irritated and somewhat embarrassed.

'Well, I wouldn't say 'best',' he said through gritted teeth at Harry.

Gladys smiled to herself.

'Say, I have a crazy idea,' said Harry, pretending to think out loud.

'Oh no, not another one,' mumbled Jack to himself in dread.

'Why don't you join us for supper and you can judge for yourself?' continued Harry. 'You wouldn't mind would you, Jack?'

'Er.. no,' said Jack, unsure.

'There you go!' said Harry.

Gladys wasn't sure:

'Well... I don't think...' she stumbled.

'Ahh, come on,' urged Harry. 'There's three fish and three people, what could be more perfect? It's what the fish would have wanted.'

Gladys was still unconvinced.

'Well... it's very nice of you to offer...'

'And it's Friday!' added Harry.

'Friday?' questioned Jack in confusion.

'You know,' said Harry, 'that whole Jesus, fish on Friday, buried on Saturday, chips on Sunday, spam on Monday, type thing.'

'What?!' said Jack in bewilderment.

'Religion, Jack, religion,' emphasized Harry.

'I understand the Catholicism reference to Fridays,' interrupted Gladys, 'I am Catholic.'

'Oh, thank goodness,' said Harry with relief. He turned to Jack. 'For a minute there I thought she was a Jehovah's Witness.'

Jack shook his head in embarrassment:

'Sorry Gladys,' he said, resting his hand on the garden gate, which slowly began to swing open.

Jack fell headfirst into the pile of snow that Gladys had shovelled together. Gladys had to muffle her laughter with a hand over her mouth, while Harry continued talking as though nothing had happened:

'Yes, it's not every day the maestro gets in the mood for cooking,' he said with pride.

Jack picked himself up:

'Sorry, I didn't realise your gate swings both ways,' he said, awkwardly.

'Bisexual?' asked Harry, in confusion.

'What?!' said Jack.

'Nothing,' replied Harry and quickly turned to Gladys. 'So, how about it? Jack's cooking really shouldn't be missed. Trust me, you won't be disappointed, Bori...'

Jack stamped on Harry's toes.

'B-BOY! You won't be disappointed, Gladys,' continued Harry, and gave Jack a dirty look.

Gladys was highly amused by the Jack and Harry 'double act'. She pondered for a moment, and finally was tempted.

'Are you sure you don't mind, Jack?' she asked.

'Oh, absolutely,' said Jack with apprehension, 'it would be a real... challenge.'

'Great!' said Harry excitedly. 'That's settled then. Come over at seven, for taste buds in heaven!'

'Okay,' said Gladys. 'Thank you. See you at seven.'

'Seven,' said Jack, worriedly. 'Yes. Look forward to it.'

As Jack and Harry made their way over to Jack's house, Gladys could hear their conversation.

'"You never even caught nothing", Harry?' asked Jack, questioning Harry's English again.

'Not a sausage, Jack, you were there.'

Gladys put her head in her hand, wondering what she had let herself in for.

Chapter 28

It had been over half an hour that Harry and Jack had stood numbly over a chopping board - the three untouched fish staring them in the face.

'You must be able to do something with them?' wondered Harry.

'Nope,' replied Jack, shaking his head blankly.

'Well, have you got any cook books?'

'Nope,' replied Jack, again shaking his head.

'Got it! The internet!' said Harry, excitedly. 'Full of ideas and recipes!'

'Terrific. I'll nip out and buy a computer then, shall I?'

'Oh,' said Harry, his excitement short lived. 'Do you need a computer for the internet?'

'Rumour has it.'

Another moment passed as they stood staring at the fish in defeat.

'So,' said Harry, 'what is the internet exactly?'

'Harry, we have a guest arriving in less than two hours,' said Jack, growing increasingly worried, 'and she's expecting a fish meal to die for.'

'Okay, okay,' said Harry, assertively. 'First thing we need to do is see what ingredients and spices you've got in your cupboards.'

'Good idea,' agreed Jack, hurrying to a nearby cupboard.

'Excellent, now we're getting somewhere,' said Harry, slapping his hands together.

Jack opened the cupboard doors and began rummaging through its contents.

'So what have we got?' asked Harry.

'Err, let's see,' said Jack, looking at the labels, 'Marmite, strawberry jam, maple syrup, English mustard, custard powder, vinegar, brown sauce, tomato sauce, tobasco sauce, curry paste, box of crackers, and chocolate buttons. There's also some grated cheddar, milk, butter and a dozen eggs in the fridge.'

Harry screwed up his face with uncertainty:

'Perfect!' he suddenly said. 'You grab a bowl and mix it all together.'

'What?!' said Jack in bemusement. 'You can't mix this lot together, it will taste vile!'

'Really?'

'Yes! Can't we just use the butter?'

'No, no, no,' said Harry, mockingly, 'this needs to be cordon bleu cooking; butter, indeed.'

'Well, we can't use all of this,' insisted Jack.

'Okay,' said Harry in placation, 'so take out the chocolate buttons and... the crackers, and maybe the jam... Use your imagination!!'

'Harry, no matter how hard I 'imagine', I'm never going to be a cordon bleu chef!'

'Now that's just defeatist, Jack.'

'Is it, Harry? I thought it was realistic.'

'Jack, how do you know you can't cook until you try?'

Jack stopped to think:

'Can't argue with logic like that,' he said, numbly.

'Now it's not rocket science; everything in moderation,' explained Harry with a broad smile.

'Moderation,' repeated Jack, nodding his head gently, but unsure.

'Good,' said Harry, animated. 'Now you grab a bowl get cracking with the marinade. I'll decapitate these blighters.'

'Right!' said Jack.

'Oh, and have you got any power tools?'

'Power tools?'

'I'm going to have to get into them somehow, Jack, they're still frozen.'

'I have a microwave, Harry.'

'Yes, your hair looks lovely.'

'What?!'

'Never mind,' said Harry opening the microwave door, 'I'll nuke them in your electro magnetic fish transporter.'

Jack shook his head in despair and began hunting for a bowl.

A short while later, Jack was standing over the kitchen table with a large white bowl and all the ingredients from the cupboard and fridge laid out in front of him. He hadn't a clue what he was doing, but was uncalculatingly shoving unmeasured amounts of the ingredients into the bowl and mixing them with a wooden spoon. Harry was standing at the sink using an electric sander to descale the fish. Jack broke an egg into the bowl and added a few drops of tobasco sauce, followed by a spoon of English mustard. He stirred it vigorously and lifted the spoon up to take a look at its consistency. It was very runny and Jack screwed his face up at it. He then started adding the curry paste and brown sauce. Harry brought the beheaded fish over to Jack.

'How are we looking?' asked Harry.

'Pretty good,' replied Jack, sarcastically.

'Is it ready?'

'I suppose so,' said Jack, unsure.

'The fish are ready.'

'Have you gutted them?'

'Yeah,' replied Harry, 'I told them they can't watch any TV.'

'What?' said Jack, unamused. 'Have you cut them open and pulled all their guts and stuff out?'

Harry screwed up his face in disgust:

'Isn't that the best part?'

'No, Harry, that's the crap that needs to be removed.'

'Oh,' said Harry, deep in thought. 'I seem to remember the fishmonger saying he did something like that.'

'That's alright then,' said Jack, relieved.

'I'm sure he was talking about the fish; although I didn't see his wife today.'

'We'll have to keep an eye on him then,' said Jack, playing along with Harry's dry sense of humour, 'there could be something fishy going on.'

'Stop it Jack, you're giving me a haddock.'

'Enough with the fish puns,' said Jack, looking curiously at the fish. 'I trust you've scaled them?'

'I climbed all the way to the top, Jack,' said Harry with a wink and a smile.

'Hmm,' groaned Jack.

Harry placed the fish into the bowl and Jack turned them by hand in the marinade.

'How do we cook them, Harry?'

'What are our options, Jack?'

'Er.. fried, grilled, baked, steamed or boiled.'

'Boiled?' cringed Harry.

'In boiling water.'

'Ohhhhh,' said Harry, sarcastically. 'Thank you, Delia. Steaming sounds quite avent-guard.'

'Very Jamie Oliver,' agreed Jack. 'But I haven't got a steamer.'

'Oh,' said Harry with disappointment, 'is there a special gadget to do that then?'

'Yes,' replied Jack in disbelief. 'A steamer. Did you think you just hold the fish over a boiling kettle?'

Harry contorted his face:

135

'Na, that doesn't sound right,' he replied.

'No,' emphasized Jack. 'So the choices are fried, grilled or baked.'

'Let's do them then!'

'What do you mean 'them', Harry?'

'A bit of each, Jack,' replied Harry. 'In the pan, under the grill and bung 'em in the oven! What could go wrong?'

'What indeed?' worried Jack.

Forty-five minutes later, the smoke alarms were going off and the kitchen was dense with smoke exuding from the oven. All the windows were open and Harry was trying to waft the acrid smell away using a tea towel. Jack grabbed the oven gloves and opened the oven door. He pulled out the smouldering baking tray and placed it on the table. He then helped Harry waft away the smoke until the alarms stopped sounding. Harry and Jack were coughing and spluttering, the sound of the alarm was still ringing in their ears.

They looked anxiously at the three scorched, and shrivelled, rainbow trout.

'Think they're done?' asked Harry.

'Hard to tell,' replied Jack.

'Proof of the pudding; go on try a bit.'

'Oh no, Harry; I'm the chef,' said Jack, 'I couldn't possibly be a fair judge. You try a bit.'

'Damn!'

'What's up?'

'I just remembered,' said Harry, 'I'm a vegan.'

'Since when?'

'Since you asked me to try a bit.'

'Oh.'

The men stared at the fish in bewilderment.

'Jack,' said Harry, calmly.

'Harry?'

'Where's the nearest chip shop?'

'Corner of St George's street.'

'I'll be back in twenty minutes.'

'Right!' said Jack, puffing out his cheeks with relief.

'You get rid of the stench,' said Harry, hastily leaving.

Jack looked at the fish in confusion:

'Stench? I thought they were trout?'

He picked up the tray and threw them out of the kitchen window and onto the snow in his back garden.

Chapter 29

It was 7 o'clock on the dot when the doorbell rang. Jack had dressed to impress, looking very smart in a freshly ironed shirt and tie, and wearing his best cologne. He was also a bundle of nerves as he opened the door. Gladys was looking stunningly beautiful; dolled up in her new dress and her hair styled and coloured. She was wearing a radiant smile.

'Gladys,' said Jack, his breath taken away, 'you found it okay then?'

'Err yes,' replied Gladys, playfully, 'I stopped for directions a few times. But...'

'Sorry, that was a stupid question,' said Jack, embarrassed. 'You look... wow!'

'Thank you. You look quite snazzy yourself.'

'Thanks,' said Jack, gorping. 'Yes, I'm all snazzed up and nowhere to go,' he joked.

Jack couldn't take his eyes off Gladys and was momentarily lost for words.

'Bit cold out here, Jack,' said Gladys, timidly.

'Bit hot where I'm standing,' mumbled Jack, numbly. 'Come in, come in,' he said, snapping out of his trance-like state.

Jack showed the way into the lounge where Harry,

himself looking very smart, was holding an unopened bottle of wine. The table was immaculately laid with Jack's best plates and silver cutlery. Christmas decorations and twinkling lights around the walls added the finishing touches to the room. Harry was taken aback by Gladys' beauty.

'Gladys Wilde,' said Harry in awe, 'you look a million dollars - can you lend me a fiver?'

'Sorry, I didn't bring my purse,' replied Gladys.

'I think Harry was joking,' said Jack, nervously, 'at least, I hope he was.'

Gladys smiled at Jack:

'I had a feeling.'

'Can I take your coat?' asked Harry.

'She's not wearing a coat,' said Jack, agitated.

'Then can I take your dress?'

'Harry?!' said Jack, tensely. 'Sorry about that, Gladys; I'm afraid Harry has a rather dry sense of humour.'

'And a rather dry bottle of Merlot,' added Harry with a smile. 'Wine, Gladys?'

'That would be nice. Thank you,' she replied.

'Three quid a glass,' said Harry, popping the cork.

'I see this will be a fun evening,' said Gladys with raised eyebrows.

'Will you excuse me a moment,' said Jack, 'I'm going to check on the food.'

'You're going to spit on what?' asked Harry.

''Check', Harry, I'm going to 'check' on the food,'

replied Jack, giving Harry a dirty look before leaving the room.

'Thank heavens for that,' said Harry, pouring the wine. 'For a minute there, I thought we were going to have a spit roast.'

Harry handed a glass of wine to Gladys.

'Are you going to charge me for this?' she asked.

'Naaaa,' replied Harry. 'You can work it off in the kitchen later.'

'Well, Merry Christmas,' said Gladys, raising her glass.

'Good health,' said Harry, raising his.

Gladys took a sip:

'Mmm, nice drop,' she said.

'He chose it himself.'

'Red wine with white fish?'

'Red, white, blue - you know what it's like with those creative bods like Jack; the rule book goes out of the window.'

'Does it now?' said Gladys, impressed.

'Of course; that's why he is such a genius in the kitchen. There are no rules.'

'Whatever you say, Harry.'

'Please take a seat, Gladys - there will be no charge,' said Harry, sliding a chair out for Gladys at the dining table.

'Thank you,' said Gladys, accepting the chair.

At that moment, Jack reappeared looking apprehensive.

'Ah! Here's the man,' said Harry. 'What was it you used to say about cook books, Jack?'

'Er... I can't remember,' replied Jack, nervously.

Harry tut-tutted and then reminded him:

'"Cook books" he used to say, "I'd rather shut my w...."'

'Willy!' shouted Jack, nervously jumping in. 'I mean will you like to eat now? I mean, it's ready, and best while it's hot... I say.'

Gladys laughed:

'Well, let's not let it go cold then, I say.'

'Yup,' agreed Harry, 'wheel it in, Jack, we're bloomin' starving, I say.'

'Coming right up,' said Jack, leaving the room again.

'I'm quite looking forward to this,' said Gladys.

'I can't wait,' mumbled Harry and lifted his glass again. 'Merry Christmas.'

'Cheers,' replied Gladys.

Meanwhile, outside in Jack's back garden, a cat had found the fish, thrown out by Jack earlier, and was sniffing around it.

Inside the lounge; a strange smell emanating from the kitchen, caught Gladys' attention.

'Something wrong?' asked Harry.

'Strange aroma,' replied Gladys.

'Do you like it?' asked Harry, knowing full well it

was the stench of the burnt fish - which Harry and Jack had tried their best to waft away and decided to camouflage with air freshener.

'Bit unusual.'

'Bloody horrible, if you ask me,' said Harry. 'I made Jack go upstairs and take another bath - all that cheep cologne he splashes on. I gave him some proper stuff.'

'Good for you,' said Gladys, unsure if Harry was joking again.

'I'll open a window,' said Harry.

Jack wheeled in a silver trolley with three covered plates resting on top. Gladys was apprehensively excited.

'Ah, Jack, we were just talking about you,' said Harry, opening a small window and returning to the table.

'Nothing horrible, I hope,' worried Jack.

'I'll smell you, later,' chortled Harry.

Jack nervously placed a plate down in front of Gladys and lifted the lid:

'Voila!' he said, dramatically.

Gladys' face dropped - on the plate she saw a battered fried fish, chips and peas, looking remarkably similar to that served up at Freddie's Fish Bar in the centre of town.

Outside in Jack's back garden, two more cats had joined in sniffing around the fish and a scuffle for the food had begun.

Inside, Gladys was politely eating and Jack and Harry were tucking in when the cat fight could be heard just outside, increasingly getting louder and more fierce. Gladys flinched with every cry. Jack and Harry completely ignored it.

'This is unbelievable, Jack!' said Harry, kissing his fingertips with approval. 'Perfection. What do you call it?'

'Err, Fish... chips... and... peas,' replied Jack, sheepishly.

'Genius!' said Harry. 'Got any ketchup?'

Outside, another cat had joined in the fight for the fish. The cat's fierce screams and cries echoed throughout the neighbourhood.

Gladys was getting edgy, the cat fight clearly affecting her.

'Remarkable how you've managed to get the trout tasting just like... cod, Jack,' she said teasingly, trying to distract herself from the activities outside.

'Is there no end to the boy's talent?' said Harry, proudly.

Jack lowered his head with embarrassment and ate even quicker.

'That cat fight is getting a bit loud,' said Gladys with concern.

'Yes,' agreed Harry, 'where's that cat burglar when you need him?'

'Cat burglar?' wondered Gladys.

'Yes,' said Jack, 'bizarrely, he was stealing all the cats in the area,'

'Oh,' said Gladys, 'hasn't done a good job, has he?'

The cat cries were getting piercingly loud and Gladys' flinching was intensified:

'Would you mind if we close the window?!' she asked, loudly, over the commotion.

'Good idea! Keep the moths out!' said Harry. 'And talking about bugs; do you know last night, I got bitten three times?'

Jack was frantically shaking his head at Harry - not wanting him to continue the story.

'Three times!' emphasized Harry. 'Once on my arm...'

Jack was growing increasingly worried - he shook his head more vigorously.

'Once on my leg...' continued Harry.

Panic was starting to set in; Jack had his fist in mouth, biting hard on his knuckles and looking daggers at Harry.

Harry continued with his story:

'And once right on the end of my...'

'NOB!!' shouted Jack.

At that moment, the cat fight suddenly stopped - all went deathly silent. Jack was horrified with what he had just said. Gladys was struggling not to laugh out loud, whilst Harry leant back in his chair wearing a smug grin.

Jack nervously smiled and quickly picked up a butter dish:

'...of butter anyone?' he asked, pretending to finish the sentence.

Later that evening, Harry and Jack were showing Gladys to the door.

'Well, that was a very entertaining evening, Jack,' said Gladys, earnestly. 'Sorry I couldn't stay any longer - wine and food makes me tired.'

'Don't apologize, Gladys,' said Harry, his voice slightly slurred. 'Where I come from there's a saying.'

Gladys politely waited to hear the saying. Harry struggled to remember it, contorting his face in puzzlement, and in the end just smiled gormlessly.

'That's okay,' said Jack, 'we've got a whole heap of washing up to do.'

'Absolutely,' agreed Harry. 'Come Gladys, I'll show you where Jack keeps the rubber gloves... in his bedside cabinet.'

'Thank you, Harry,' said Jack, rolling his eyes.

'Well, good-night then,' said Gladys, and gave Jack a peck on the cheek.

'Good-night, Gladys,' said Jack in a daze.

'Night!' shouted Harry.

As Gladys made her way back up the garden path, she suddenly stopped when she spotted the tail end of a trout that the cats had been fighting over lying in the snow. She looked at it and smiled knowingly. She turned to Jack:

'Give my regards to Freddie,' said Gladys.

'I will,' replied Jack, who was still on cloud nine from the kiss and didn't get the obvious reference to the Fish Bar.

Gladys waved and continued her short journey home, leaving Harry and Jack smiling and waving on the doorstep.

'I wonder who Freddie is?' pondered Jack.

Harry started to put on his coat:

'How the hell should I know?' he replied.

'Where are you going? I thought you were staying here?'

'I am,' replied Harry. 'I just wanna see what Gladys was looking at.'

Harry stepped outside and Jack followed him.

'She kissed me, Harry,' said Jack, still floating.

'Are you still going on about that?'

'I won't wash my cheek, ever; I can still smell her.'

'You're not gonna break into song again, are you?'

'I'll tell you something else...'

'Something else?' asked Harry in dismay. 'You haven't told me anything yet. Now what's this thing Boris was looking at?'

Harry started scanning the floor, but was too drunk to spot anything.

'After the food fiasco,' continued Jack, 'I spent a

whole evening with Gladys and I didn't do anything stupid.'

Just at that moment, Jack's front door closed - *BANG!* locking them out.

'Hmm,' groaned Harry. 'Well, I'm off home.'

Harry began staggering up the garden path.

'You're not gonna leave me out here are you?' asked Jack, in distress.

'You'll be okay,' said Harry, 'you left the kitchen windows open, remember?'

'I might need a bunk up!'

'Not on your first date, Jack; have some respect.' Harry continued to stagger away.

Jack sighed in disbelief at being deserted. He braced himself in the cold and headed down the side of the house.

Chapter 30

The following morning, David and his family had come to visit. Jack was sitting at the kitchen table in his dressing gown and slippers, still pondering on the events from the night before and wryly smiling as he remembered the kiss that he had received from Gladys. David was peering into the cupboard and was puzzled.

'Dad, where's all the food gone?' he asked.

'Oh,' replied Jack, in a haze, 'I ate it.'

'Ate it?' said David, miffed. 'Yesterday there was a full jar of jam... and marmite! And... loads of other stuff.'

'I was hungry,' said Jack, playing innocent.

'No kidding,' said David.

Mandy was looking in the fridge:

'The fridge is empty as well,' she said with surprise. 'You must have been starving, Dad.'

'And what is that awful fishy smell?' said David, in disgust. He opened the back door to let some fresh air in.

Jack started to waft his hand behind his backside:

'Yeah, sorry about that,' he said, jokingly. 'You know how it is - old people and... bottoms.'

He winked at Lance, who started laughing.

'Disgusting!' said David, who grabbed an air freshener from the window sill and started spraying the kitchen.

'Don't worry, Dad,' said Mandy, reassuringly, 'we'll pop out and get you some more supplies.'

'Thanks, Mandy,' said Jack.

'Well, we'd better go now then,' said David.

'You've only just got here,' said Jack, mystified.

'It's a few days 'til to Christmas, Dad,' emphasized David, 'the shops are going to be ram-packed!'

Mandy started rummaging through Jack's dirty washing. She lifted up a shirt:

'How on Earth did you do this, Dad?' she asked, staring at a large rip across the chest.

'Oh, just a little accident,' replied Jack.

'What little accident?' asked David, with concern.

'Climbing through a window,' replied Jack with an edge.

'Why?' asked David.

'For the over 60's, Christmas, window climbing competition,' replied Jack, growing increasingly irritated.

'Dad?' groaned David, unamused and getting angry.

'I locked myself out, David!'

'How?' asked David, worried that his Dad could be going senile.

'It was easy,' replied Jack, and started explaining it in a mocking manner – as though he was talking to a four-year-old. 'I went outside... shut the door... and

150

then realized I didn't have a blooming key! How do you think it happened?!'

Lance started laughing. Mandy was also highly amused:

'Lucky you left a window open, Dad,' she said.

'Oh, I always leave a window open,' he said, glaring at David, 'in case I can't be bothered to use the door. Sometimes I leave the front door open to remind me to close the windows.'

'You're impossible!' said David in despair.

Jack took the opportunity to wind his son up further:

'Yesterday,' he continued, 'I went out and left a trail of breadcrumbs - to remind me to buy a loaf of bread on the way home.'

'Ha.. ha,' said David, straight-faced.

'Are you coming over to us today, Granddad?' asked Lance.

'Oh, sorry, Lance, but I've got today reserved,' answered Jack.

'What are you up to?' said David with suspicion.

'You know, normal, senile type, elderly things,' replied Jack.

'With Harry?' wondered David.

'Possibly,' replied Jack, deep in thought. '... I forget.'

'I hope you remembered - we won't see you Christmas Day, Dad,' said Mandy, 'we're driving over to my parent's house.'

'I know,' said Jack, 'but I'll see you on Boxing Day,

won't I?'

'Yes, we'll be home,' said Mandy.

'I can pick you up,' said David.

'Don't worry, David, I'll make my way there.'

'Are you sure you're gonna be okay on your own on Christmas Day, Granddad?' asked Lance with concern.

'Of course I am,' said Jack reassuringly.

'Okay, let's get the shopping out of the way,' said David, heading for the door.

'Bye, Dad,' said Mandy, kissing Jack on the head.

'Good bye, Granddad; love you,' followed Lance, giving Jack a big hug.

'Love you too,' said Jack. 'See you all later.'

The family departed, leaving Jack sitting alone in the kitchen. He slowly leant back in his chair and smiled, reminiscing about 'the kiss' again. He was floating on cloud nine until:

'Oh crap!' he said, suddenly realising Gladys' reference from the previous night. 'Freddie!' he exclaimed, burying his head in his hands.

Chapter 31

Later that morning, Jack and Harry were out walking again, along a quiet snowy country lane, heading towards the open countryside.

'Do you know where I think you went wrong, Jack?'

'I went wrong, Harry? I got a kiss.'

'Peck on the cheek, Jack; you can get that just by saying 'hello' in France - in fact you'll get two in Italy, one on either cheek.'

'I feel short changed now.'

'In parts of Scandinavia, you can't even look at a girl without getting a snog.'

'Really?' said Jack, intrigued, 'whereabouts?'

'On the mouth, Jack; we're not talking Holland here, you know.'

'Well, we're not in any of those countries.'

'Shame,' said Harry with disappointment. 'Anyway, back to Boris. You didn't woo her enough, Jack; women love to be wooed - The wooeder the better.'

'I wined her and dined her, Harry.'

'And pretended you cooked it.'

'Well, whose idea was that then?'

'Details, Jack, details,' said Harry, brushing it aside.

'Fish and chips is hardly 'dining' a girl, Jack.'

'I suppose not,' said Jack, downtrodden.

'Although, it's amazing what you can get from a girl if you buy 'em fish and chips on a Friday night in Newcastle.'

'You really are a man of the world, Harry.'

'I'd like to think so,' agreed Harry, feeling self satisfied. 'You see, a woman like Boris needs to be showered in gifts; she needs to be told how adorable she looks and how wonderful she smells.'

'Harry, where the hell are you getting all this from?'

'Life, Jack, life,' said Harry, pondering wisely. He then added, with an over exaggerated expression of emotion. 'I know women - I know how they feel and what they need. I sense their passion and insecurities. I know what drives them and makes them tick.'

'Sorry, where?' asked Jack.

'Some magazine at the hospital.'

'Oh,' said Jack, despairingly.

They sat down on a bench overlooking the view of the snow-topped countryside and hills shimmering in the midday winter sun.

'Isn't it breathtaking, Harry?'

'Spectacular, Jack.'

'Sends a shiver down my spine.'

'Yeah, it is a bit nippy,' said Harry, producing his small silver flask. 'Here, this will help,'

He unscrewed the lid and passed it to Jack.

'Cheers,' said Jack taking a swig.

The men spent a moment absorbing the Christmas card setting view.

'Harry, do you ever think about things you wished you'd done when you were younger?'

'Clearly you have, Jack,' said Harry, taking back the flask.

'Think about them a lot since that little heart scare,' explained Jack.

'You can't go through life with regrets, Jack,' said Harry, philosophically. 'It's not healthy.'

'I know - I keep telling myself that. But it's not easy,' said Jack, despondently. 'Part of me feels... unfulfilled; empty. Don't you have regrets?'

'Only that I didn't wear two pairs of socks.'

'Seriously, Harry?'

'Seriously, Jack; my feet are like ice blocks,' said Harry, taking a large mouthful of brandy.

Later, Jack and Harry were back rambling through the countryside snow.

'So what are these things you regret not doing, Jack?' wondered Harry.

'Oh, silly things really.'

'What's to stop you doing them now?'

'Age, Harry, age.'

'Age is just a state of mind, Jack.'

'And a knackered body.'

'Okay, so the body's not working as good as it used

to,' agreed Harry. 'But why would that stop you fulfilling a few dreams?'

''Cos one of them is to play centre forward for England.'

'Ladies netball?'

'Football, Harry; men's football.'

'Oh... yeahhh... think I've heard of that,' said Harry. 'So you've never fancied women's netball?'

'Never.'

'Shame.'

Harry suddenly spotted something:

'Look!' he called out.

'What?' asked Jack, wearily.

'There!' said Harry, pointing.

In the distance there was a wooden barn.

'A barn; thank heavens we're saved!' said Jack, sarcastically.

'I could be wrong, Jack...'

'It has been known, Harry.'

'...but isn't that Sam Holden's Barn, where he keeps that prize winning cotton ball of his?'

'Oh yeah,' said Jack, excitedly. 'What are you thinking, Harry?'

'I'm thinking we should have brought some mint sauce,' replied Harry with an evil glint. 'Follow me.'

'You're not going to eat Stallion, are you?' asked Jack with a sly grin.

'Don't be silly,' replied Harry. 'I'm a vegan, Jack. Remember?'

Harry led the way across a field and through thick snow. They managed to climb under a wired fence and headed towards the barn, laughing uncontrollably all the way.

It was later that afternoon when Sam went to check on his prize winning sheep. He pulled open the barn door:

'Where are you my darling?' he said, impatiently. 'Daddy's here to see you.'

Upon entering, Sam sensed that something wasn't right.

'Stallion?' he said, tentatively walking inside.

He suddenly stopped dead in his tracks - his heart sank, he was filled with horror. His beloved sheep, Stallion, was standing in the corner, happily bleating, but he had been sheared bald. Sam then noticed that his three cows, on the other side of the barn, were all wearing comical wigs - made from the sheared fleece of Stallion. Sam fell to his knees and looked up to the heavens:

'NOOOOOOOOOOOOOOO!!!!!!!!!!' he cried.

Chapter 32

It was early evening. Jack was at home, anxiously pacing the lounge floor, trying to psych himself up. He was holding a small bunch of flowers and a small box of chocolates, meant for Gladys. He was desperately trying to find the words to go with them:

'Gladys, I can't apologise enough... No, no,' he said, changing his mind for the umpteenth time. 'My dear Gladys, I feel I should explain my pretence... No. Ms Wilde, last night you may have noticed that I wasn't entirely... No!' he said, getting annoyed with himself. 'Gladys, yesterday I made a complete arse of myself... Arse?' he questioned in bewilderment, 'you can't say 'arse' in front of a lady.'

Jack paused for a moment deep in thought before starting up again: 'My dearest Neighbour, please accept these gifts as a token of my remorse and deep regret, that I... I... am a bloody liar. ARGH!' he yelled, looking up to the heavens in frustration.

He paced the room hitting the flowers gently against his head. 'No, no, no, no,' he said, angrily. He stopped and took in a deep breath. 'Gladys, I'm sorry... yes that's it!' he exclaimed. 'Plain and simple; I'm sorry, Gladys.'

Jack left his house, brandishing the chocolates and flowers, still quietly rehearsing to himself:

'I'm Sorry, Gladys... Gladys, I'm so sorry.'

He had only walked a few paces up his garden path when he stopped. Heading jauntily down Gladys' garden path was a short stout man, in a very smart suit, carrying an enormous bouquet of flowers and a king-size box of chocolates, beautifully gift wrapped in a red bow. Jack was taken aback, unsure what to do. The stranger spotted Jack:

'Merry Christmas,' he said with a broad, unnerving smile.

Jack quickly hid his embarrassingly tiny peace offering behind his back.

'Merry Christmas,' replied Jack, numbly in a lacklustre tone.

The man reached Gladys' front door and rang the bell. Jack instinctively ducked down behind his garden wall.

As the man waited at the doorstep, he looked around, somewhat surprised to see that the neighbour had vanished, but he didn't dwell on it for long; his smug, broad smile quickly returned. He pulled his jacket by the lapel and sniffed his armpit odour with satisfaction and then adjusted his tie. Gladys opened her door and was unpleasantly surprised to see a face she vaguely remembered:

'Oh,' she said looking down at a man, three quarters her size, 'Mr Marrow?'

'That's right, Andrew Farrow - Merry Christmas!' he said holding out the gifts.

'Merry.. Christmas,' said Gladys, befuddled, 'you really shouldn't have.'

'Nonsense; it's the least I can do to repay you for such a wonderful evening we spent together.'

Jack had overheard - his heart slowly sank.

Gladys' recollection of the evening was very different, and Andrew turning up on the doorstep she found awkward.

'Thank you,' she said, reluctantly accepting the gifts.

'Can I come in?' asked Andrew, beaming. 'I won't stay long.'

Gladys couldn't find it in herself to refuse.

'Er.. yes,' she said, hesitantly.

Jack was devastated. He slid to the floor with his back up against the garden wall, staring despairingly at the menial gifts in his hands.

Chapter 33

The following day, Jack and Harry were casually strolling along another quiet and snowy country lane.

'So,' said Harry, begrudgingly, 'what's so urgent that you had to drag me away from scratching my backside?'

'Harry, I've got an adversary.'

'What, a wedding adversary?'

'A rival, Harry!'

'Arrival? What are you, an airport?'

'I'm serious, Harry; I took your advice…'

Harry stopped and turned to Jack:

'Jack, you shouldn't go around listening to an old man's advice.'

'But you said…?'

'Uh uh uh!' said Harry, interrupting and holding up a finger, sternly. '<u>Old man</u>,' he emphasized.

Jack rolled his eyes and continued walking: 'Anyway,' he said, with a fleeting look at Harry in despair, 'I got Gladys the biggest bunch of flowers… that I could find… in the 'reduced' bucket,' he said, sheepishly, 'and an enormous.. normal-ish size.. box of Dairy Milk and went 'round there to woo her.'

'You sure know how to treat a lady, Jack'.

'But then, after psyching myself up for two hours,' continued Jack, 'I was on my way there only to find that she was already being wooed - by someone else!'

'That's a bit wooed,' said Harry, offended.

'Damn wooed,' agreed Jack. 'To make matters worse...'

'It gets worse?'

'Oh yes,' said Jack. 'The wooer was a pint sized man, no bigger than... my arm!'

'Now Jack, think hard; are you sure you weren't just looking at him from a distance?'

'No Harry, he was tiny! So small, that the box of chocolates he was carrying was completely disproportionate to the size of his body; he may have been carrying chocolates the size of a fridge.'

'So you think they were bigger than yours?'

'Yes, Harry,' said Jack in a daze, 'there's a possibility they were <u>much</u> bigger than mine.'

'Ahh,' said Harry, nodding his head in recognition, 'the age old problem every man has wondered; is his nut cluster bigger than mine.'

'I wish I'd never gone 'round there,' said Jack, demoralized.

Harry suddenly shuffled to a halt and grabbed Jack by the shoulders:

'Great Scott! If we don't stop Gladys and Danny DeVito getting together, this could have grave consequences for your children in the future!'

'Thank you, professor,' said Jack with a deadpan

expression.

Harry released Jack and gave him a friendly pat on the shoulder.

'So, how do we stop them, Harry?'

They carried on walking.

'Hard one, Jack,' said Harry pondering, 'he sounds cute.'

'He's adorable,' said Jack through gritted teeth.

'Then maybe you should just give him a biscuit, tickle him under the chin and send him on his way.'

'He's cute, Harry – not a puppy.'

'Okay,' said Harry, assertively. 'So what do we know about him?'

'His name is Andrew Farrow and…,' said Jack, his voice wavering, 'I heard him say that he spent a wonderful night with Gladys.'

'Wonderful?' repeated Harry, his mind racing.

'His very words,' replied Jack, downtrodden.

'Crafty little chap, isn't he?'

'Well, he's small,' replied Jack, 'he can get in all the little nooks… and grannies.'

'Hmm,' said Harry.

'Harry, there is a Christmas fair in town.'

'Is that where he escaped from?'

'What?'

'The freak show - with the bearded lady.'

'It's a Christmas fair,' said Jack in bewilderment, 'not a 1930's circus.'

'Oh,' said Harry with disappointment, 'I thought we

could just return him.'

'Not an option,' said Jack. 'But I also heard Farrow say that he's going to the fair tonight with Gladys.'

'The fair, you say?' said Harry, deep in thought.

'And he particularly loves the dodgems.'

'Excellent, so my plan is coming together.'

'What plan, Harry?'

'No time for idle chit-chat now,' replied Harry, his eyes lighting up.

Heading towards them, wheeling a shopping trolley, was a sweet little old lady returning from her Christmas shop.

'I do believe that's Elsie Botherington, desperately trying to cross the road,' continued Harry.

'Oh yeah,' said Jack with a sly grin.

Chapter 34

That evening, Harry and Jack arrived at the winter fair - a Christmas spectacular event that attracted young and old from miles around. There were exhilarating highflying rides, a beautiful mythical animal-themed carousel, Santa's grotto where children could meet elves, fairies, reindeers, goblins and Santa Claus himself. The fair included a Yuletide Market selling an array of unusual, unique and handmade gifts. There were wooden chalets selling hot chocolate and mulled wine and a vast array of foods from traditional German sausages to pancakes and crêpes. There were colourful stalls selling candy floss, doughnuts and popcorn. In the middle of the fair was the centrepiece; an ice rink surrounded by exquisite ice sculptures of forest animals. Christmas songs and carols were heard throughout the fair. It was a winter wonderland with a magical Christmas atmosphere - everyone was having fun, that was, except Harry and Jack. They were looking as hard as nails as they walked through the fair, focused and determined - men on a mission. They were looking out for Gladys and Andrew en route to the dodgem ride.

'How are we supposed to find 'pint-size' amongst all

these children?' wondered Jack.

'No Jack,' said Harry in bemusement, 'look out for Gladys.'

'Good idea.'

'Not such a strain on the old neck,' explained Harry, 'and besides, the munchkin's probably been mistaken for an elf and has been abducted into Santa's grotto.'

'Stop trying to cheer me up, Harry.'

As they soldiered on through crowds of meandering people; they were just passing the food stalls when Jack suddenly stopped:

'Uh oh,' he said with alarm, 'bandits at 12 o'clock.'

'What?' said Harry, baffled, 'is that the midnight headlining act or something?'

'No,' said Jack, 'it's Sam!'

Up ahead, the giant figure of Sam Holden was heading their way. Sam looked lost and miserable, desperate to unload his emotions on anyone that would listen to the story of his prize-winning sheep.

'What do we do?' asked Jack in a panic.

'Quick,' said Harry, dragging Jack by the arm, 'follow me.'

Harry led Jack towards the food stalls and they hid themselves amongst a crowd of people queuing up for food.

A short while later, Harry and Jack reappeared from the stalls with their faces hidden behind giant pink candyflosses. They had only walked a short distance when Ray Hargreaves mysteriously appeared in front of them.

'Hello Harry, Jack,' he said coolly.

Harry and Jack slowly lowered their candyflosses, miffed that they had been recognised.

'Hello Ray,' said Jack.

'Hi Ray,' said Harry, somewhat embarrassed.

Ray put a pipe to his mouth and pressed down the tobacco with his thumb.

'I see you boys still have a sweet tooth then?' said Ray.

'Not really,' said Jack, 'it's supposed to be a disguise.'

'Oh,' said Ray, 'very impressive. I take it by your 'disguises' that Sam Holden must be here somewhere?'

'Yes,' replied Jack.

'Oh,' said Ray.

Ray casually lit his pipe and took a few puffs, while Harry and Jack waited patiently.

'Surprised he's here,' said Ray in bemusement, 'have you heard the news on Sam?'

'No,' replied Harry.

'No,' replied Jack, apprehensively.

'He's gone stark raving mad, you know?' said Ray, coolly.

'Tell me more,' said Harry with a smile.

'Claims his cows ganged up on Stallion,' continued Ray.

'You're kidding?' said Jack.

'Apparently,' said Ray, seemingly unfazed, 'two held Stallion down whilst another cow shaved him bald.'

Harry and Jack sniggered with amusement.

'The cows then used the fleece to make themselves wigs,' said Ray with raised eyebrows. 'A classic case of mad cow's disease, he reckons.'

'Oh, absolutely,' agreed Harry.

'The only explanation,' said Jack.

Ray took a couple of puffs of his pipe then calmly added:

'So Sam shot them all.'

Harry and Jack were taken aback and stood in stunned silence. Ray took another puff of his pipe.

'I'll be off then,' he said, calmly. 'Better get myself one of those candyfloss disguises,' and he casually started to walk away.

'Yeah,.. bye Ray,' said Harry in a daze.

'See ya, Ray,' said Jack, numbly.

Harry and Jack looked at each other, dumbfounded.

'I wasn't expecting that,' said Jack.

'Never mind,' said Harry, regaining his determination, 'we've got a Smurf to find.'

Clutching the candyflosses in front of their faces, for fear of bumping into Sam again, they marched their way through a sea of people and eventually arrived at the dodgems.

'This is it,' said Jack.

'Well spotted,' said Harry, glaring out at the track.

He aggressively ripped off a piece of candyfloss with his teeth and started to chew - promptly spitting it out.

'What is this?' he said, turning his nose up at it in disgust.

'Sugar on a stick,' replied Jack, scanning the area.

'Sugar on a stick?' repeated Harry, miffed.

'Yes, pink sugar on a stick.'

'Oh, yum,' said Harry with a dead-pan expression.

'Look!' said Jack, tensely. 'There she is!'

Gladys was seated on the other side of the dodgems track watching the cars going around. She was looking bored and somewhat embarrassed -discreetly looking around, hoping that she would not be spotted by someone she knew.

Harry and Jack simultaneously threw their candyflosses high into the air, over their shoulders. Then, like a couple of cowboy western bandits, they pulled their scarves up over their faces with just their eyes showing.

'Okay,' said Harry, 'that means the Oompa Loompa is in one of these cars.'

'I'm on it,' said Jack, peering at the track.

There were twenty colourful electric cars travelling anticlockwise around the track. There was mood lighting with the occasional flashes of simulated lightning bolts and loud music which every so often, would dip down in volume for an announcement:

'*Bumping is not allowed. Please do not bump the cars.*'

Jack was scrutinising each car that passed, until he eventually spotted Andrew - and there could be no mistake; he was driving his bumper car wearing the same unnerving smile that he had the day Jack met him.

Jack's eyes narrowed:

'I see him,' he said, grinding his teeth.

'Good,' said Harry, cracking his knuckles.

The ride ended; the music died down and the cars came to a halt. People were stepping out of their cars, being replaced by those in the waiting queue. Andrew's car had stopped close to where Gladys was waiting. She was anxiously up on her feet, but Andrew was having the time of his life. He clutched the steering wheel tightly:

'Gladys, one more go!' he called out, his face beaming with excitement.

Gladys despondently rolled her eyes. She shrugged her shoulders and forced an approving smile in Andrew's direction.

'Yes!' said Andrew, his heart racing with anticipation - eager to set off again.

Gladys reluctantly sat back down, clearly jaded.

Before long, the dodgems were off; the loud music started up, the mood lighting switched on and the cars were whizzing around the track. Andrew was pretending to be Formula One racing driver Lewis Hamilton as he weaved his way through the cars in front. Gladys was cold and tired. She watched Andrew with tedious boredom and superficially waved at him every time he passed.

On the third lap, there was a small pile up of cars in front, and Andrew found himself caught up on the side. An announcement came on:

'Bumping is not allowed. Please do not bump the cars.'

As Andrew tried to move, he glanced across to see two cars going the wrong way around the track and heading straight towards him. Andrew started to panic, pressing on the accelerator, but wasn't able to move.

An announcement came on again:

'Bumping is not allowed. Please do not bump the cars!'

Gladys could see what was happening and was up on her feet.

Andrew was filled with horror as the two masked men driving the stray cars suddenly rammed his car side-on - *WHACK!!*

Chapter 35

Later that evening in Jack's house, David and close family friend, Dr Stephen Pollard, were sitting in the lounge staring at Jack in disbelief. Jack was sitting in a reclining armchair with his leg elevated and a bandage on his knee. His left wrist was also bandaged and there were a few minor scratches on his face.

'You did what?' asked David.

'I had a slight mishap,' replied Jack, coyly, '...in a bumper car.'

'Bumper car?' repeated David in despair.

Jack ashamedly nodded his head:

'You know, dodgems – except I didn't.'

'Dad, you could have killed yourself.'

'Don't be silly, David,' said Jack, smirking, 'the cars only go a few miles an hour. Besides, I had protection.'

'Protection?' laughed David, nervously. 'He had protection. What, were you wearing a condom?'

'No, I was wearing a seat belt,' replied Jack, 'and I thought those things were fitted with airbags.'

'Airbags?' repeated David looking up to the heavens. 'Tell me I'm not hearing this?'

'Okay,' admitted Jack, 'so I was joking about the airbags.'

'Dad, you've had serious heart problems!' said David, losing his cool. 'Your heart is extremely fragile; what the hell were you doing at the Christmas Fair?!'

'Well, Harry and I....'

'Harry!! I should have known.'

'Don't blame Harry, I'm the one that dragged him along. I wanted to go on the dodgems.'

'Well, that's great! That's just great! Next you'll be telling me that you went on the Ghost Ride!'

'I'm not that stupid, David.'

'Really?'

'No!... They didn't have a ghost ride.'

'So did you try the roller coaster instead?'

Jack feigned a shiver running down his spine:

'Oooo I'm never going on that again, I can tell you. Scared me half to death - whoops wrong expression.'

David jumped out of his seat:

'That's it, go to your room!!' he yelled, pointing a finger upstairs.

'David, HELLO, this is my house,' said Jack, 'I'm your Dad.'

'I give up, I've had it with this man!' said David, pulling his hair out. 'He needs locking up!'

'Okay, calm down David,' said Dr. Pollard.

'You talk to him!' raged David, 'I need some air.'

'That's a good idea,' said Dr. Pollard.

David left the room in a huff and Jack pouted again like a school boy.

'Have I upset him?' asked Jack, sarcastically, over

exaggerating his sad eyes.

Stephen couldn't help but smile:

'What are we going to do with you, Jack?'

A few hours later, David and Dr. Pollard had gone, leaving Jack alone on the reclining chair with his bandaged leg still elevated. Jack looked miserable. He sighed heavily as he flicked through the TV channels not really wanting to watch anything. The door bell suddenly rang - *DING DONG*. Jack turned the TV off and struggled to his feet:

'Oh, ya bugger,' he said in pain, as he put weight on his injured knee.

He managed to hobble along the hallway and opened the front door - it was Harry, looking rather nervous:

'Is the coast clear?' he asked, checking over his shoulders.

'How should I know?' replied Jack, 'we don't live anywhere near the sea.'

'Good,' said Harry with a devilish smile, 'I've brought some pain killers.'

Harry held up a bottle of rum and two giant Havana cigars.

'You better come in then,' said Jack with a broad grin.

Jack and Harry were leaning out of the upstairs bedroom windows smoking the cigars and drinking rum. Jack took a big puff:

'Ohhh, heaven' he said, blissfully. 'How sad is it that we have to smoke out of a window, just in case my son finds out?'

'Pretty sad,' replied Harry, downing a glassful of rum.

'For crying out loud; this is my house, Harry!' said Jack in frustration. 'Can't I do what I want in my own home?'

'Absolutely, Jack, Shall we go downstairs and smoke in the lounge?' asked Harry with raised eyebrows.

Jack thought for a moment:

'Better not,' he said, cowering. 'David might pass by tomorrow.'

'Oh, right,' said Harry, sardonically.

'Not that I'm scared of him!' insisted Jack.

'Of course not,' said Harry continuing to mock.

'Maybe, I should start calling him Dad,' mumbled Jack, quietly to himself.

'Oh look,' said Harry getting animated.

'What?'

'Boris must be getting ready for bed.'

'What?!' said Jack, who was up like a shot and limping swiftly over to Harry's side of the window.

'Move over,' said Jack, anxiously. 'Move over.'

Jack put the cigar between his teeth and hung out of the window as far as he could. The light was on in the bedroom upstairs and Gladys appeared at the window.

'Oh, yeah,' said Jack, his heart skipping a beat.

Harry also put his cigar between his teeth and the pair stood watching, with eyes wide open.

Gladys walked passed the window several times, removing her jumper. Then she stopped, in full view, and started to undo the buttons on her blouse.

Jack's heart started racing - the cigar suddenly fell from his mouth and into his wide open shirt.

'AHHHH!' he yelled in a panic.

He jumped back inside, frantically rummaging down his top for the cigar.

'Hmmm,' said Harry, spellbound. 'You say something, Jack?'

Jack was jumping around like a lunatic, undoing his shirt buttons and trying to retrieve the lit stump.

At the window, Gladys was undoing more buttons and Harry watched with a huge gormless smile, his cigar still between his teeth.

Jack managed to find the cigar and was frantically brushing away black ash from his chest:

'What'd I miss, Harry? What'd I miss?'

'Hmmm?' said Harry, lost in another world.

Jack was anxious to return to the window, but just as he approached, without looking, he put the cigar back in his mouth - lit end first. He instantly spat it out - straight back into his shirt.

'Oh, for crying out loud!' winced Jack, back inside the bedroom and jumping around like a lunatic again.

'Knickers! Knickers! Knickers!' he cried, as he

rummaged for the cigar.

Gladys' blouse was undone - her bra showing. Harry was mesmerised. But Gladys drew the curtains and Harry's face dropped. He let out a sigh of disappointment.

Jack had found the cigar. He brushed himself down and hurriedly limped back to the window with black ash around his lips.

'What happened?!' asked Jack, anxiously.

'I've seen better,' replied Harry, blasé, and turning away from the window.

Jack peered out and noticed that Gladys' bedroom curtains were drawn. He winced - extremely jealous of Harry.

'What were you getting so excited about, Jack?'

'Blooming cigar!' said Jack with annoyance, throwing it out of the window. 'It should carry a health warning.'

Jack wiped his mouth and went back inside to examine his burnt stomach.

'Hmmm, so, Mr Flatly,' said Harry folding his arms, 'how's the knee, after that Riverdance routine?'

'Never felt... worse,' said Jack, staggering towards his bed. He sat down and lifted his injured leg up onto it. 'Doc says I have to do a minimal amount of walking on it for the next day or so - to get the swelling down on the knee.'

'Oh,' said Harry with disappointment. 'Bummer.'

'Yeah,' agreed Jack, despondently. 'So I reckon I'm

grounded for Christmas - which should keep David happy. Although he won't be really happy 'til I'm in a home.'

'A home for the mental-knee handicapped?'

'Yes, Harry; that's the one,' said Jack, collapsing backwards onto the bed.

'Well, I'll leave you in peace, my friend,' said Harry, heading for the door.

'Yeah. Night, Harry. Thanks for the painkillers.'

Chapter 36

It was early Christmas Eve morning at the hospital. Harry was stripped to the waist and standing behind the screen of an x-ray machine. The 53-year-old nurse operating the machine was straight-faced and humourless. Harry was his normal and cheerful self.

'Ok, hold please,' said the nurse in a dull, monotone voice, ready to take the first x-ray shot.

Harry did a stupid grin <FLASH>.

'One more to the side,' said the nurse.

Harry turned to the side and did another stupid grin <FLASH>.

'Are you sure these are okay for passports?' asked Harry.

'No, Mr MacDonald,' said the nurse, 'you'll have to go to the Post Office for those.'

'Oh, really?' said Harry, mystified at the nurse's lack of humour.

'One of the back, please,' said the nurse, ready for the next x-ray.

Harry moved into position, then turned his head back towards the nurse and did another stupid grin <FLASH>.

'Yeah, but I don't think they're open on a Tuesday,' continued the nurse.

'Thank you,' said Harry, 'you really are a little bundle of knowledge.'

'Not really, it just so happens my husband is a postman,' explained the nurse. 'You can put your shirt back on, Mr MacDonald.'

'Husband?' wondered Harry. 'What a lucky man he is.'

'Not really,' said the nurse, with no grasp of sarcasm, 'although he did once win £10 on the lottery.'

'Well,' said Harry, putting his shirt back on, 'I hope he spent it wisely.'

'It's 'Wiley', Nurse 'Wiley',' she corrected.

Harry continued to dress, shaking his head in bafflement.

Moments later, Doctor Stephen Pollard was looking at Harry's x-rays. Harry was seated close by.

'Give it to me straight, Doc,' said Harry, 'how long have I got?'

'How long would you like?' said Dr. Pollard with a smile.

'Really?' said Harry, calmly with surprise, 'I'll take 50 years then, if you're offering it on the National Health.'

'Seriously, Harry; your one lung seems to be functioning fine,' assured Dr. Pollard.

'No sign of the dreaded 'C'?' asked Harry in

astonishment.

'Nope,' replied Dr. Pollard, 'so far so good, but we'll keep doing regular checks.'

'I think this calls for a celebration,' said Harry getting to his feet.

'Now don't overdo things, Harry.'

'What things are these, Stephen?'

'Whatever it is you're about to overdo,' said Dr. Pollard sternly with raised eyebrows.

'Oh, those things,' said Harry, sarcastically, and headed towards the door.

'Harry, I know you've been through a lot,' said Dr. Pollard, sympathetically, 'but you're doing just fine – you really don't need to live each day like it's your last.'

Harry paused to think. Then, with a cheeky smile, he winked and opened the door to leave.

'Have a great Christmas, Doc,' said Harry departing.

'And you, Harry,' said Dr. Pollard, with a feeling that his words had fallen on deaf ears.

A few minutes later, Harry was cheerfully walking at pace along the high road near the town centre. Every other old lady that passed was fearfully keeping their distance. But Harry merrily smiled and tipped his hat at them all; greeting them with:

'Hello Mrs Botherington...' 'Lovely to see you, Mrs Botherington…' 'Ah Mrs Botherington...' 'You're looking well, Mrs Botherington…'

Harry had passed several large shops and showrooms, all plastered with 'Christmas Sale' banners and stickers, when he suddenly stopped - wearing a mischievous grin.

Chapter 37

Jack was looking extremely fed up, seated in front of the TV with his injured leg elevated. He was still in his dressing gown and slippers. He was starting to doze off when the sound of a car horn outside awoke him - *BEEP! BEEP! BEEP! BEEP!* This was followed by the excessive revving of a car engine.

'What the hell?' said Jack, annoyed.

The revving and car horn continued - *BEEP! BEEP! BEEP! BEEP!*

'For crying out loud', groaned Jack, struggling to his feet. As he limped towards the front door, he grabbed an umbrella – intending to use it as a weapon. The noise was relentless - *BEEP! BEEP! BEEP!*

'Bloody kids!' said Jack, throwing open his front door in anger.

It was a bright and cloudless day outside. The sun was reflecting off the snow causing Jack to squint. The noise of the car engine revving was deafening and it was coming from directly outside of Jack's house. Jack shielded the sun from his eyes and hobbled outside, swinging the umbrella above his head, and headed for the silhouetted vehicle. He managed to get to the end of his garden and was about to launch an attack with the brolly when he stopped in mid-swing – staggered by what he saw: The noisy car was a brand new, out of the showroom, gleaming metallic blue convertible Mercedes sports car with the top down. Sitting in the driver's seat wearing dark shades and the broadest of smiles was Harry.

'For goodness sake, Jack,' said Harry, bewildered. 'What the hell do you want a brolly for in this weather?'

Jack was gobsmacked. He accidentally pressed a button, opening the umbrella above his head:

'To keep the bloomin' sun off, what else?' he replied, and stood gorping at the car in awe.

'Okay, Mary Poppins; go get some clothes on,' said Harry, excitedly, 'we're going for a ride!'

A short while later, Jack reappeared fully dressed. As he approached the Merc, Harry slid over to the passenger seat.

'What are you doing?' asked Jack.

'I assume you wanna drive?' answered Harry, dangling the car keys in his hand.

'I'm not allowed to drive.'

'Fine,' said Harry, unbothered, 'I'll drive then.'

Harry started to move back towards the driver's seat when Jack opened the driver's door:

'Oh no you don't,' he said climbing in, 'Give me those keys!'

Jack jumped in and snatched the keys from Harry.

He made himself comfortable in the seat and started the engine:

'Oh, music to my ears,' he said in ecstasy as he revved the engine.

'Sweet as a whistle,' agreed Harry.

Jack adjusted the rear-view mirror:

'Right, where are we heading?' he asked, energized.

'Good question,' replied Harry and pondered for a second. 'The beach! Let's go to the beach!'

'Really? On a day like this?' fretted Jack.

'We're not going to sunbathe, Jack, we're going for a ride,' said Harry with grit.

'Beach it is!' said Jack, enthusiastically. 'Are we going with the top down?'

'Why not?' replied Harry, 'the sun's out, there's no wind, it's a glorious winter's day.'

'You're right, Harry.'

'Oh,' said Harry, suddenly remembering, 'I got you these.'

Harry handed Jack a pair of black Ray-Ban sunglasses.

'Excellent,' said Jack, and slipped them on.

Jack gripped the steering wheel and sat poised ready to go. He revved the engine, focused and determined:

'It's 120 miles to Beachy Head, we've got half a tank of four star unleaded, a bag of humbugs, it's daytime and we're pensioners.'

'Hit it!' said Harry.

Jack put his foot down. The Merc did a wheelspin in

the snow before speeding away. It had only reached the end of the road when Jack said:

'Actually, Harry, I think I need the toilet first - I'm busting.'

'Oh for goodness sake,' despaired Harry.

'Sorry, Harry,' said Jack, wimpishly, 'I had no idea how exciting this was going to be.'

After a short toilet break, the Mercedes was back on the road, speeding through a dual carriageway across the countryside. Harry was having the time of his life, cheering at the top of his voice:

'WOOOO! This is the life, Jack!'

Jack, on the other hand, was shaking from the cold and looking in considerable discomfort:

'Harry!' he shouted, 'I can't feel my hands.'

'It's an automatic, Jack; just keep them on the steering wheel.'

'I couldn't move them if I tried, said Jack, 'they're frozen on!'

'Well, there you go,' said Harry, contently, 'problem solved.'

'My face is so cold - my lips are turning blue!'

'Goes with the car,' said Harry, grinning.

'Can we please shut the roof?!' pleaded Jack.

'For goodness sake Jack, I thought you wanted an open top convertible?'

'For the summer, Harry,' said Jack, his teeth chattering, 'for the summer!'

'Oh,' said Harry, disillusioned. 'Okay,' he said, begrudgingly giving in. 'But first you have to let me do something.'

'Uh oh,' said Jack with dread.

A family car was travelling along a quiet open country road. Inside, David was driving, Mandy was in the passenger seat, while Lance was in the rear, looking bored, sitting amongst a mass of shopping.

'Are you sure we've got everything?' asked David.

'I think so,' replied Mandy, 'I've bought enough food to last Dad a whole week.'

'Good, cos I'm not going back for anyone,' said David with an edge, 'the shops are hell.'

'Well, it is Christmas,' Mandy reminded him, 'and he is your Dad.'

'He's a pain in the backside,' mumbled David.

'Poor man must be depressed sitting at home all day,' said Mandy with empathy, 'No wonder he's eating so much.'

'I wish that were true, Mandy; but he keeps going walkabouts!' said David in bewilderment.

'He's hardly going to do that now, not with his dodgy knee,' said Mandy.

'I bloomin' hope not,' muttered David, 'he's driving me insane; and he's only got himself to blame.'

'Oh, come on David, don't be so hard,' reasoned Mandy. 'It can't be easy being old and helpless. Your Dad has been through a lot. It's Christmas, have a heart.'

Mandy's words had pulled on some emotional strings. David calmed and started to feel guilty:

'Yeah, you're right,' he said, ashamedly. 'Look, maybe we should spend a little time there instead of just dropping this stuff off and leaving.'

'That would be nice,' said Mandy, with a smile.

'Look Dad!' shouted Lance, pointing at something ahead.

A convertible sports car was heading towards them at speed. The passenger was standing up with his arms held out in the crucifixion position.

'What's that idiot doing?!' asked David, taking his foot off the accelerator.

Lance was highly amused. He wound down his window and poked his head out to take a better look. As the car approached, Lance's face lit up with excitement:

'It's Uncle Harry!' he shouted.

'What?' said David, puzzled.

'And Granddad!!' yelled Lance.

As the convertible Merc whizzed past, David and Mandy watched with mouths agape, witnessing that it was indeed Jack at the helm and Harry standing, with arms outstretched, both yelling at the top of their voices:

'WOOOOOOOOOOOOOOOOOO!!!'

'Oh.. my.. God!' said David in shock. He slammed on the brakes and screeched the car to a halt at the side of the road.

Lance was laughing out loud and jumping up and down in his seat, while Mandy held her head in her hands, open mouthed in disbelief. David dashed out of the car to take a look and watched in shock as the Merc sped off into the distance.

)

Chapter 38

Harry's Mercedes was parked, with the roof down, near the cliff top at Beachy Head. There were no roads or people in sight, just a clear stretch of snow-covered land and the tyre tracks leading to Harry's car.

Jack and Harry were standing near the cliff's edge looking out to sea. It was a bright and sunny afternoon. There was a cold light breeze drifting in from the sea. The view was spectacular.

'Wow,' said Jack, 'this is amazing.'

'I'd say,' agreed Harry in awe.

'Why would anyone want to go abroad, when they have all this in their back yard?'

Harry was baffled by the question:

'Hot weather, cheap booze, topless totties and all night raves,' he replied.

'Oh yeah,' said Jack, 'forgot about that.'

A moment passed as they stood watching the view.

'We really should go to Spain next summer, Harry,' said Jack.

'Absolutely,' agreed Harry.

Harry removed his shades, closed his eyes and tilted his head back - soaking in the suns rays:

'It's been a great Christmas so far, hasn't it Jack?'

he asked.

'Are you kidding?' replied Jack in bemusement, 'I've had heart problems, reprimands, rejections, dinner disasters, bumbling encounters, drunken embarrassments; I've had to escape through a pub toilet window, tangle with a love rivalling midget, burnt myself on the chest with a cigar – not to mention a collision in the dodgems and a knackered knee - which is killing me, in case you're interested.'

'But it's been good, hasn't it?' beamed Harry with a devilish smile.

Jack removed his shades. He also closed his eyes and tilted his head towards the sun and smiled.

'Yeah, it's been a scream,' replied Jack.

'So where are we with Boris?'

'Boris?... Nowhere, sadly' said Jack, melancholy, 'I've blown it there.'

'I think she likes you.'

'Harry, in case you've forgotten, we tried to assassinate her date.'

'And we would have succeeded, if it wasn't for that pesky munchkin – calling an ambulance out... for you.'

'Alright, you don't have to rub it in,' said Jack, fed up.

'She helped you into the ambulance, you know,' said Harry.

'Really?' said Jack, glancing over to Harry, 'you never mentioned that to me before.'

'It was when they were administering the oxygen –

she picked up your hearing aid.'

'That wasn't my hearing aid!'

'She wasn't to know that,' explained Harry, 'although it would explain why she kept calling your name when you weren't responding.'

'She was calling my name?!'

'She thought you were hard of hearing.'

'I was out of it!' snapped Jack.

'Whatever you say, Jack.' said Harry, placating, and smiling to himself.

Jack sighed and puffed out his cheeks in bewilderment:

'You didn't think to tell her, Harry?' he said softly.

'Me?' replied Harry, innocently. 'I was too busy growling at the little fellow... and picking up your humbugs.'

Jack let out a nervous laugh:

'Humbugs,' he repeated, in a daze.

'Well, I knew you liked them,' said Harry, teasingly.

'Oh God,' said Jack looking up to the heavens and shaking his head in dismay, 'this is even worse than I thought.'

'Well, I still say you're in with a shout... which is probably the only way you're gonna hear her,' joked Harry.

'Will the deaf puns never end?' sighed Jack in dismay. 'This is so humiliating.'

Harry looked over to Jack:

'I say she likes you, Jack,' he said, earnestly.

'Harry, I appreciate that you've been trying your damndest to get us together, but she has a boyfriend, remember?'

'Nonsense, you're twice the man Pint-size could ever be – no pun intended,' said Harry.

'No pun taken,' replied Jack.

'Boris likes you, Jack,' emphasized Harry in a serious tone.

Jack let out a heavy sigh:

'Well, I don't know what more I can do,' he said, despairingly.

'You'll think of something,' said Harry, putting his shades back on.

They stood in silence for a few moments looking out to sea.

'Harry, do you think there's life after death?' asked Jack.

'What the hell brought that on?' wondered Harry.

'I don't know; we're both getting older and have health issues.'

'Life is too short to think about death,' said Harry, nonchalantly. 'You're not scared of dying, are you, Jack?'

'I don't know,' replied Jack. 'What if there isn't an afterlife, Harry? What if there's nothing, an eternity of nothing when we die? What if this is it, this is all we get and there is nothing more?'

'Bloody hell, Jack; that was a bit deep for a

Tuesday,' said Harry with surprise. 'You really are afraid of dying, aren't you?'

Jack gently nodded his head:

'I suppose,' he answered, ashamedly.

'I wish I could answer your questions,' replied Harry with empathy. 'But I guess we won't know 'til we get there.'

'I guess,' agreed Jack. 'Why aren't you afraid, Harry?'

'Because I'm too stupid to be afraid,' replied Harry with a wry smile.

'I had my suspicions.'

'But if I go before you, Jack, and there is an afterlife, then I promise I'll do my damndest to come back to let you know.'

'You'll come back and haunt me?' asked Jack, worriedly.

'Something like that.'

'Cheers, Harry, you're a real pal,' said Jack sarcastically.

'No problem,' said Harry. 'You know, all that talk of death has made me thirsty.'

'Me too; fancy a pint?' asked Jack.

'Thought you'd never ask,' replied Harry.

Harry took hold of Jack's arm and assisted him as he limped back towards the car.

Chapter 39

It was late afternoon on Christmas Eve, when Gladys opened her front door and was surprised to see Jack leaning unsteadily against a wooden post near her front doorstep.

'Jack; I wasn't expecting to see you up and about.'

'Hello Gladys,' said Jack, timidly.

'I hope you didn't touch anything on the way in?' said Gladys, peering outside.

Gladys was looking as glamorous as ever and Jack was finding it hard to focus on anything but her looks. 'Only the ground, mainly with one leg,' replied Jack, captivated.

'I was joking, Jack.'

'Oh,' said Jack.

'How is the knee?'

'The knee?' asked Jack in a daze.

'Yes, how.. is.. the.. knee!' shouted Gladys, slow and deliberate.

'Umm, painful,' replied Jack. 'And Gladys, you don't have to shout, I'm not deaf.'

'Oh,' said Gladys, surprised, 'but I found your…'

'That wasn't my.. I mean..' fumbled Jack, 'I've got that from… What I'm trying to say is… I'm cured!' he said, thinking out loud and immediately regretted saying it.

'I see,' said Gladys, highly suspicious, 'so the bang on your knee cured your hearing?'

'No,' said Jack, cringing, 'I'm getting all befuddled.'

'Well, calm down,' said Gladys. 'Would you like to come in?'

'Err, no.. thanks,' replied Jack, coyly.

'It's okay, I've nailed everything down.'

'I don't think I should. I just need to apologize.'

'Apologize?' said Gladys, raising her eyebrows.

'Look, cards on the table,' said Jack, psyching himself up, 'I can't cook, I can't fish, I can't seem to do anything in front of you without making a complete idiot of myself.'

At that moment, Jack's legs slipped from under him on the icy footpath. He managed to catch himself from falling, but accidently booted an empty milk bottle against the garden wall - *SMASH!*

From out of nowhere, a startled stray black cat screeched with a loud shrill across Jack's foot.

'Ahh!!' said Jack, flinching in shock.

'I hadn't noticed,' said Gladys with a deadpan expression.

'But there's more,' said Jack, trying to regain his composure.

'I don't think I can take any more,' said Gladys.

'You know that little… I mean that small… I mean that misfortunate... incident yesterday?' said Jack, fumbling for words again.

'Do you mean Andrew?'

'Yes,' replied Jack, 'that's the little… I mean, tiny.. er.. titchy.. small incident.'

'Yes,' said Gladys, pondering sarcastically. 'I do seem to remember something,'

'Well,' said Jack, his voice croaking, 'it wasn't exactly an accident.'

'No?' asked Gladys, taken aback.

'No,' said Jack, sheepishly.

'It's chilly out here, Jack; perhaps you'd better come in and start explaining.'

A short while later, Gladys and Jack were sitting at the breakfast table in Gladys' kitchen. Gladys was pouring tea from a china teapot into matching teacups.

'I hope this is not your best set?' fretted Jack.

'It's old, but not worth much - if you're thinking of drop-kicking it against the wall,' replied Gladys.

'I just don't know what it is,' said Jack in bafflement. 'I have some sort of… selective company Tourette's.'

'Interesting: Only around me, you say?'

'Yes,' said Jack, wearily.

'Now, mind yourself Jack, I like my tea extremely hot,' said Gladys, passing Jack a cup.

'Thank you,' said Jack, and spotted the biscuits. 'Ah Digestives,' he said, grabbing one from the plate. He snapped it in two and dunked one half in his tea.

'I hope you don't mind me asking, Jack...'

'Not at all,' replied Jack.

'You don't know what I'm going to ask yet.'

'Oh... sorry,' replied Jack, awkwardly.

'About a month ago, I saw an ambulance pull up outside your house,' said Gladys with concern, 'I saw them take you away - you looked in pretty bad shape.'

'Oh, that!' said Jack, brushing it aside as something trivial.

'You don't have to talk about it if you don't want to,' assured Gladys.

'No, that's okay,' said Jack, unbothered. 'It was just the old ticker.'

'Oh, no,' said Gladys, worriedly.

'Ahh, it was nothing; it missed a few beats for a while.'

'And there was me thinking it might have been serious,' said Gladys, sarcastically.

'Naa,' said Jack, lifting the dunked biscuit up from the cup only to find that most of it had melted off. 'Oh,' he said, looking at the remainder of the biscuit floating in the tea cup.

'So, did they find out what caused it?' wondered Gladys.

Jack put his fingers in the boiling tea cup to try and remove the biscuit.

'NOOOO!!!!' he yelled in agony.

He quickly removed his hand and shook it under the table, trying to hide the obvious pain, while Gladys kept a straight face - ignoring the incident.

'No,' continued Jack in a strained voice, 'they think it could be any number of things, but it's all guess work really.'

Jack grabbed a tea spoon from the table and fished out the biscuit. He looked where he could put it.

'Are you okay now?' wondered Gladys.

Jack decided to put the very hot spoon in his mouth and instantly spat it back into the tea cup:

'YESSS!!!' he cried in agony again, '...absolutely tip-top shape.'

'Would you like a drop of cold milk?' offered Gladys.

'Oh, yes, please,' implored Jack.

Gladys passed Jack a little milk jug and watched in astonishment as Jack smiled and placed his scolded fingers into it.

'Ahh, that's better,' said Jack with relief.

'Okay,' said Gladys, placing her elbows on the table and looking menacingly at Jack, 'now tell me what happened last night.'

Chapter 40

That evening, Gladys and Wendy were sitting at a table in a busy wine bar situated in the centre of town. Christmas songs were playing over the sound system and the Victorian style bar was beautifully decked out with lights and tinsel.

Gladys had been pouring her heart out to Wendy, only to find that Wendy's reaction was to have an uncontrollable laughing fit.

'What's so funny, Wendy?' asked Gladys, slighted.

'Oh come on,' said Wendy, wiping the tears of laughter from her eyes, 'are you telling me you can't see the funny side of this?'

'He was intent on ruining my evening.'

'What?!' said Wendy, baffled. 'You gave me a right ear-bashing about not wanting to go.'

'Well, I didn't,' admitted Gladys, 'but that's not the point.'

'Sounds like Jack did you a favour.'

'He did, but he had a "contract" out on Andrew.' There was a short pause; both women were desperately trying not to laugh. Wendy picked up her glass to take a drink.

'Did I mention that Harry and Jack were driving

their bumper cars wearing scarves over their faces, like bandits?' said Gladys.

Wendy spat her drink out and was in fits again, holding her sides:

'Gladys stop,' she pleaded, hurting from laughter, 'you're killing me.'

Gladys couldn't help but laugh herself:

'This is serious,' she said, chuckling, 'they tried to run him off the track.'

Wendy was falling off her chair:

'Enough! Enough!'

'If Andrew ever finds out,' continued Gladys, 'he could take them to the.. small claims court.'

Wendy fell under the table, uncontrollably laughing.

'Did I tell you about the hearing aid?'

'Enough!!' cried Wendy in agony.

Gladys buried her head in her hands:

'What a mess,' she said, laughing to herself in despair.

It took a few minutes before Wendy eventually picked herself up. Her mascara was a mess. Gladys passed her a tissue.

'Thanks,' said Wendy, damping down her eyes and still guffawing. 'Was Andrew hurt?'

'Just a little,' explained Gladys.

Wendy was off again; laughing and holding her sides:

'I'm gonna pee myself in a minute,' she cried.

'Behave yourself, Wendy,' said Gladys, chortling

along. 'You know, I'm not sure if Harry said something to Andrew, but he was trembling with fear when he was calling the ambulance.'

'And he hasn't called you since?' asked Wendy, wiping her eyes.

'No, thank goodness,' said Gladys with relief, 'he was a bit creepy, you know?'

'Sorry, Glad; I feel guilty for introducing him to you.'

'No you don't,' said Gladys with a snigger, 'you've had a jolly good laugh at my expense.'

'Well, at least something good has come out of this,' said Wendy.

'Oh really?' wondered Gladys with suspicion.

'Yes - Jack,' said Wendy, raising her eyebrows and grinning.

'Huh,' said Gladys, dismissively, 'you can forget about him.'

'Are you serious?' said Wendy in astonishment. 'I'd love to find a valiant and handsome man prepared to duel for the right of my affections.'

'What century are you living in?' asked Gladys in bemusement.

'Aren't you at all flattered?'

'No, Wendy; I'm a bit freaked out,' replied Gladys, 'they're both creepy; Jack was spying on me.'

'He overheard a conversation from next door, that's not spying.'

'He hid behind a garden wall and then, when

Andrew was leaving, he opened a window so he could hear us better.'

'For goodness sake, Gladys; this is hardly MI5 surveillance,' said Wendy in despair. 'He really likes you and thought he had competition - give him a break.'

Wendy got to her feet and grabbed her bag:

'I'm gonna clean myself up and get some more drinks,' she said with a wink and headed towards the bar.

'Okay,' said Gladys, numbly. She leant back in her chair, deep in thought.

Chapter 41

It was late night, Christmas Eve, inside The Dog & Trumpet. The pub was rammed-packed and Sam Holden could be seen sitting in the corner on his own, devastated, and drowning his sorrows.

Jack and Harry were at the bar. Jack was also looking down in the dumps, sitting with his injured leg rested up on a stool. Harry was sitting next to him, smirking. Jack had just finished telling Harry about his confession to Gladys.

'Then she sent me limping home with my tail between my legs,' said Jack, downing a large mouthful of beer. He slammed the empty glass down on the bar and looked pitiful again.

'What were you expecting to happen, Jack?' asked Harry, exasperated.

'I dunno,' replied Jack, staring aimlessly into space. 'Maybe I was expecting to be free of all my guilt.'

Harry rolled his eyes:

'And she'd forgive you, and you'd hobble off, hand in hand, into the sunset to live happily ever after,' mocked Harry.

'Something like that,' said Jack, distantly.

Stan the landlord was serving behind the bar and

had overheard:

'Here, Jack, I know the way to a woman's heart,' he said, looking serious.

'Oh, said Jack, warily, 'pray tell.'

'Well,' said Stan, 'first find her kidneys then turn left at the liver.'

'What a bundle of wisdom you are Stan,' said Jack unamused.

'But seriously,' said Stan, 'It's Christmas Eve and I don't like seeing you so sad.'

Jack was quite touched:

'Thanks, Stan, I appreciate it.'

'Yeah, so why don't you go over there and sit with Sam, so we don't have to look at your miserable faces,' said Stan with a friendly wink.

'Kick a man while he's down, why don't you?' said Jack in a daze.

'Fate worse than death,' said Harry, glancing over to Sam.

'Talking about death,' said Stan, sinisterly. 'Heard about that chap that got murdered!'

'What, here in this town?' asked Harry.

'Well, they were talking about it in the town square today,' replied Stan.

'Blimey,' said Jack, suddenly interested, 'it wasn't a little chap found dangling on the end of a rope, was it?'

'Worse!' said Stan in distress. 'They nailed this poor bloke by the hands and feet!'

'Hang on,' said Harry, 'was his name Jesus, by any

chance?'

'That's the chap!' declared Stan. 'You heard then?'

'Yeah,' said Harry with a deadpan expression, 'I think it may have been on the news.'

'Hope they catch the buggers, it was his birthday tomorrow, can you believe?' said Stan, shaking his head in anger.

'Who'd have thought,' said Jack.

Stan picked up the empty glasses:

'Same old, same old, gents?'

'Same old, same old, Stan!' came the reply in unison.

Chapter 42

It was close to midnight on Christmas Eve, when a cab pulled up outside of Jack's house. The rear doors opened and Jack staggered out.

'Are you sure you don't need help to your front door, Jack?' asked the driver.

'Naa,' said Jack, his voice slurred, 'I'm fine,' he said, waving the car away.

'Okay,' said the driver. 'Merry Christmas!'

'And to you, my good fellow!'

Jack swayed as he watched the cab pull away.

'And to all your family - a very Cabbie Christmas,' he mumbled and laughed to himself.

He turned to walk towards his house and slipped with his first step:

'Arghh!' yelled Jack, falling flat on his backside on the snow.

He sat laughing to himself for a short while, when he noticed two legs standing beside him.

'Can't remember putting those there,' he said in confusion.

His eyes followed the legs up to the face – it was Gladys: She had just returned from her night out with

Wendy.

'Oh,' said Jack, with muted surprise, 'do these belong to you?'

'Shall I help you up, Jack, or are you happy to spend the night there?' asked Gladys in a friendly manner.

'Uhmm, can I ask the audience?' joked Jack.

Gladys positioned herself behind Jack:

'Up you get,' she said, straining as she dragged Jack up to his feet.

'The trouble with too much beer, Gladys, is that it makes your bum cold.'

'Yes, I read that somewhere.'

Gladys threw Jack's arm around her neck.

'Mmmm,' said Jack dreamily, 'you smell nice.'

'Thank you,' replied Gladys as they began a slow and unsteady walk towards Jack's front door.

'You smell like buttercups in the meadows of spring,' continued Jack, drunkenly. 'I suppose I smell like a Rotterdam brothel on payday… Not that I've ever been to a Rotterdam brothel…'

'I'm sure you haven't,' said Gladys.

'…on payday,' mumbled Jack.

Gladys managed to get Jack to his front door.

'There we go,' said Gladys, releasing him.

'That's very kind of you,' said Jack, patting himself down. 'I seem to be all out of change.'

Gladys tutted and rummaged through Jack's coat pocket.

'Is this some kind of bust, Officer?' asked Jack,

staring at Gladys' chest and wearing a drunken smile. Gladys rolled her eyes and found his keys. She opened the front door.

Jack looked at Gladys amorously:

'Would you like to come in for a love bite?.. A love cap?.. A night bite?.. A bed cap?.. A bed bath?'

'Very kind of you,' laughed Gladys, 'but I'm off home.'

'You know, Gladys,' said Jack, trying to be serious, 'I'm only drinking to forget what an idiot I am.'

'Are you, Jack?' asked Gladys, hoping for an intelligible answer.

'Of course I am!' announced Jack, proudly. 'That's why I'm all alone for Christmas.'

Gladys looked at Jack for a brief moment with sympathy:

'Goodnight, Jack.'

'I'll walk you home,' said Jack, staggering inside, 'I'll just.. get my.. coat,' said Jack closing the front door.

Gladys could hear Jack softly singing:

'*Swing low, sweet chariot, coming for to carry me home…*' as he hobbled up the stairs.

Gladys shook her head in bafflement and headed home.

Chapter 43

It was Christmas Day morning and Jack was grumpily hobbling in agony along his hallway towards his front door - *DING DONG!*

'I'm coming, I'm coming,' said Jack, in a cantankerous mood - emulating Ebenezer Scrooge.

He swung open the front door and was taken aback to see Gladys: She was looking stunning, dressed in a glamorous red chiffon Christmas party dress and red stiletto shoes. There was a white imitation fur shawl draped over her shoulders and a matching fur Santa hat. She was standing under the falling snow and brandishing a beautifully wrapped gift.

'Merry Christmas!' she said, holding out the present.

'Merry Christmas,' said Jack, completely blown away. 'For me?'

'Yes, it's just something small to remember this Christmas by,' said Gladys with a cheeky grin.

Jack accepted the gift and started to unwrap it on the doorstep - too shaken to think about inviting Gladys inside from the snow.

'You really shouldn't have,' he said, tearing the Christmas paper asunder to reveal a Toy Dodgems Car

Set.

'I couldn't resist it,' said Gladys, laughing. 'All the cars are remote control, you can crash as many times as you like, Jack; and all the drivers are titchy.'

Jack started to laugh:

'I have a feeling I'm gonna really enjoy playing this,' he said in all seriousness.

'Glad you like it.'

Jack looked longingly at Gladys:

'Are you off to a party?' he wondered.

'Party?' said Gladys. 'No, not at all; I'm just... dressed for Christmas.'

'Oh,' said Jack, in a daze. 'So where are you spending the day, if you don't mind me asking?

'Home,' replied Gladys.

'Home?'

'Next door,' she replied, nodding towards her house.

'Oh, that home.'

'Yes.'

'Have you not got family?' enquired Jack, timidly.

'Yes, but they're all off doing other things,' replied Gladys.

'Same here,' said Jack, downtrodden. 'Although I wonder if they're just telling me that, to keep the old man out the way, so to speak.'

'I'm sure that's not the case,' said Gladys, reassuringly.

'Maybe not,' said Jack, wanting to believe but unsure.

'Listen,' said Gladys, hesitantly, 'are you cooking anything for Christmas dinner?'

'Cooking? You must be joking,' replied Jack, 'I still can't get rid of that stench of fish; I'm strictly an 'eat straight out of the fridge' man now.'

'Strictly?' asked Gladys with raised eyebrows.

'Well... maybe I could be swayed to bend the rules,' said Jack, sheepishly.

'I've got a turkey in the oven, with sage and onion stuffing.'

'Stuffing?' repeated Jack, his mouth watering.

'Roast potatoes, honey-glazed parsnips, Brussels' sprouts,' she continued, slow and sensually.

'Stuffing?' repeated Jack, salivating in a daze.

'Carrots, swede, peas, thick lashings of ...

'You did say 'stuffing'?' interrupted Jack.

'..gravy,' continued Gladys, 'and pigs in blankets'.

'Wow,' said Jack, dreamily, 'blanketed pigs.'

'For dessert...'

'Dessert?' repeated Jack, mouth agape.

'...I've got hot Christmas pudding, inflamed in brandy and served with double cream and brandy butter.'

'Gladys...' said Jack, going weak at the knees, 'you sound sexier than an M & S advert: Why do you torture me so?'

'Why, what are you having to eat, Jack?'

'Me?' said Jack, still in a daze. 'Bread and cheese.'

'Oh come on,' said Gladys, disbelieving.

'I like cheese,' said Jack with a sad puppy-like face.

'Well, I've got ten varieties of cheese for later this evening.'

Jack swallowed a lump that came to his throat:

'With a little cheese knife that turns up at the end?' he asked, numbly.

'Yes,' laughed Gladys, 'with a little cheese knife, curled at the end - two prongs.'

'Two prongs?' said Jack, mesmerized by Gladys' words and collapsing up against the wall, fantasising. 'Crackers?' he asked.

'Are you really, Jack?' quipped Gladys.

'Completely,' muttered Jack.

'I have six varieties… and a bottle of vintage port.'

'I think I need to lie down,' said Jack, lost in another world.

'So,' said Gladys, coyly, 'what do you think?'

'I think you're going to have the best Christmas ever.'

'No, Jack,' said Gladys, hesitantly, 'I'm alone for Christmas.'

'Me too,' said Jack, in no fit state to read between the lines. 'Life is so cruel.'

'So, if I am alone and you are alone, how about we...'

'Stay in touch?'

'No, Jack,' said Gladys, mildly annoyed, 'I'm suggesting that maybe we… spend Christmas together.'

Jack was puzzled:

'I don't know if I have enough bread, Gladys.'

'At my house!'

'Excellent suggestion! I love you.. er <u>to</u>! I'd love to!' corrected Jack.

'Good,' said Gladys with a smile, 'why don't you hop on over when you're ready.'

'I will,' said Jack. 'Oh, one thing; do you mind if I bring a friend?' he asked sheepishly.

'I thought you said you were alone for Christmas?'

'I am, but... sadly, so is Harry.'

'Oh,' said Gladys, feeling sorry for anyone having to spend Christmas alone. 'Well, what's Christmas without Harry?' she said with compassion.

'Really?'

'Why not?' beamed Gladys.

Harry suddenly appeared from behind the doorway:

'Excellent!' he said, slapping his hands together. 'Merry Christmas, Glad.' He gave her a kiss on the cheek and headed out of the door towards Gladys' home. 'I'm a breast man myself, in case you're wondering,' he said over his shoulder.

Jack closed his eyes and shook his head in embarrassment. 'Couldn't wait, could you, Harry; couldn't bloody wait,' he mumbled to himself.

'I can see this is going to be a long Christmas,' said Gladys, light-heartedly.

'Very long,' agreed Jack.

Gladys produced a twig of mistletoe from behind her back:

'Shall we use this before Harry sees it and attempts to ravish me?'

'If Harry sees that, he'll probably ravish *me*!' snarled Jack, glancing out to see where Harry was.

'So I guess it's best to 'use once and throw away',' suggested Gladys, holding the mistletoe over her head.

Jack's heart skipped a beat as Gladys stepped forward and planted a kiss on his lips.

Harry was waiting impatiently on Gladys' doorstep, shivering from the cold. He looked over and spotted the pair smooching. He tutted and rolled his eyes:

'Oh, for goodness sake,' he muttered to himself in despair before shouting: 'Oi you two!! Get a room!!

Harry tried pushing Gladys' locked front door and quietly groaned to himself. 'Preferably in here before I die of pneumonia.'

Back on his doorstep, Jack momentarily broke away from the kiss:

'Did you hear something?' he asked, in a haze.

'Not a damn thing,' said Gladys and continued the kiss.

19902845R00136

Printed in Great Britain
by Amazon